In The Beginning...

Books bombarded Montag's shoulders, his arms, his upturned face. A book landed, almost obediently like a white pigeon, in his hands, wings fluttering. In the dim wavering light a page hung open and it was like a snowy feather, the words delicately painted thereon. In all the rush and fervor, Montag had only an instant to read a line, but it blazed as if stamped there with fiery steel.

And then Montag's hand closed like a mouth, crushed the book with wild devotion, with an insanity of mindlessness to his chest. Montag had done nothing. His hand had done it all . . . his hand, with a brain of its own, with a conscience and a curiosity in each trembling finger, had turned thief.

Montag knew it was madness, suicide— but it was also a beginning!

Fahrenheit 451

Ray Bradbury

Fahrenheit 451—
the temperature at which book paper catches fire, and burns . . .

A Del Rey Book

BALLANTINE BOOKS • NEW YORK

A Del Rey Book
Published by Ballantine Books

Library of Congress Catalog Card Number: 53-11280

ISBN 0-345-32032-8

Manufactured in the United States of America

U.S. Printing History
First Edition: October 1953
Sixty-first Printing: June 1984

Canadian Printing History
First Edition: February 1963
Seventh Printing: October 1972

Special Editions
Asbestos Edition: October 1953
Revised Bal-Hi Editions
First Printing: January 1967
Tenth Printing: October 1973
Special Book Club Edition: March 1976

Cover art by Barron Storey

This one, with gratitude,
is for
Don Congdon

CONTENTS

If they give you ruled paper,
write the other way.

Juan Ramón Jiménez

PART ONE

The Hearth and
the Salamander

It was a pleasure to burn.

It was a special pleasure to see things eaten, to see things blackened and *changed*. With the brass nozzle in his fists, with this great python spitting its venomous kerosene upon the world, the blood pounded in his head, and his hands were the hands of some amazing conductor playing all the symphonies of blazing and burning to bring down the tatters and charcoal ruins of history. With his symbolic helmet numbered 451 on his stolid head, and his eyes all orange flame with the thought of what came next, he flicked the igniter and the house jumped up in a gorging fire that burned the evening sky red and yellow and black. He strode in a swarm of fireflies. He wanted above all, like the old joke, to shove a marshmallow on a stick in the furnace, while the flapping pigeon-winged books died on the porch and lawn of the house. While the books went up in sparkling whirls and blew away on a wind turned dark with burning.

Montag grinned the fierce grin of all men singed and driven back by flame.

He knew that when he returned to the firehouse, he might wink at himself, a minstrel man, burnt-corked, in the mirror. Later, going to sleep, he would feel the fiery smile still gripped by his face muscles, in the dark. It never went away, that smile, it never ever went away, as long as he remembered.

He hung up his black beetle-colored helmet and shined it; he hung his flameproof jacket neatly; he showered luxuriously, and then, whistling, hands in pockets, walked across the upper floor of the fire station and fell down the hole. At the last moment, when disaster seemed positive, he pulled his hands from his pockets and broke his fall by grasping the golden pole. He slid to a squeaking halt, the heels one inch from the concrete floor downstairs.

He walked out of the fire station and along the midnight street toward the subway where the silent air-propelled train slid soundlessly down its lubri-cated flue in the earth and let him out with a great puff of warm air onto the cream-tiled escalator rising to the suburb.

Whistling, he let the escalator waft him into the still night air. He walked toward the corner, thinking little at all about nothing in particular. Before he reached the corner, however, he slowed as if a wind had sprung up from nowhere, as if someone had called his name.

The last few nights he had had the most uncertain feelings about the sidewalk just around the corner here, moving in the starlight toward his house. He had felt that a moment prior to his making the turn, someone had been there. The air seemed charged with a special calm as if someone had waited there, quietly, and only a moment before he came, simply turned to a shadow and let him through. Perhaps his nose detected a faint perfume, perhaps the skin on the backs of his hands, on his face, felt the temperature rise at this one spot where a person's standing might raise the immediate atmosphere ten degrees for an instant. There was no understanding it. Each time he made the turn, he saw only the white, unused, buckling sidewalk, with perhaps, on one night, something vanishing swiftly across a lawn before he could focus his eyes or speak.

But now tonight, he slowed almost to a stop. His inner mind, reaching out to turn the corner for him, had heard the faintest whisper. Breathing? Or was the atmosphere compressed merely by someone standing very quietly there, waiting?

He turned the corner.

The autumn leaves blew over the moonlit pavement in such a way as to make the girl who was moving there seem fixed to a sliding walk, letting the motion of the wind and the leaves carry her forward. Her head was half bent to watch her shoes stir the circling leaves. Her face was slender and milk-white, and in it was a kind of gentle hunger that touched over everything with tireless curiosity. It was a look, almost, of pale surprise; the dark eyes were so fixed to the world that no move escaped them. Her dress was white and it whispered. He almost thought he heard the motion of her hands as she walked, and the infinitely small sound now, the white stir of her face turning when she discovered she was a moment away from a man who stood in the middle of the pavement waiting.

The trees overhead made a great sound of letting down their dry rain. The girl stopped and looked as if she might pull back in surprise, but instead stood regarding Montag with eyes so dark and shining and alive that he felt he had said something quite wonderful. But he knew his mouth had only moved to say hello, and then when she seemed hypnotized by the salamander on his arm and the phoenix disc on his chest, he spoke again.

"Of course," he said, "you're our new neighbor, aren't you?"

"And you must be"—she raised her eyes from his professional symbols "—the fireman." Her voice trailed off.

"How oddly you say that."

"I'd—I'd have known it with my eyes shut," she said, slowly.

"What—the smell of kerosene? My wife always complains," he laughed. "You never wash it off completely."

"No, you don't," she said, in awe.

He felt she was walking in a circle about him, turning him end for end, shaking him quietly, and emptying his pockets, without once moving herself.

"Kerosene," he said, because the silence had lengthened, "is nothing but perfume to me."

"Does it seem like that, really?"

"Of course. Why not?"

She gave herself time to think of it. "I don't know." She turned to face the sidewalk going toward

6

their homes. "Do you mind if I walk back with you? I'm Clarisse McClellan."

"Clarisse. Guy Montag. Come along. What are you doing out so late wandering around? How old are you?"

They walked in the warm-cool blowing night on the silvered pavement and there was the faintest breath of fresh apricots and strawberries in the air, and he looked around and realized this was quite impossible, so late in the year.

There was only the girl walking with him now, her face bright as snow in the moonlight, and he knew she was working his questions around, seeking the best answers she could possibly give.

"Well," she said, "I'm seventeen and I'm crazy. My uncle says the two always go together. When people ask your age, he said, always say seventeen and insane. Isn't this a nice time of night to walk? I like to smell things and look at things, and sometimes stay up all night, walking, and watch the sun rise."

They walked on again in silence and finally she said, thoughtfully, "You know, I'm not afraid of you at all."

He was surprised. "Why should you be?"

"So many people are. Afraid of firemen, I mean. But you're just a man, after all . . ."

He saw himself in her eyes, suspended in two shining drops of bright water, himself dark and tiny, in fine detail, the lines about his mouth, everything there, as if her eyes were two miraculous bits of violet amber that might capture and hold him intact. Her face, turned to him now, was fragile milk crystal with a soft and constant light in it. It was not the

7

hysterical light of electricity but—what? But the strangely comfortable and rare and gently flattering light of the candle. One time, as a child, in a power failure, his mother had found and lit a last candle and there had been a brief hour of rediscovery, of such illumination that space lost its vast dimensions and drew comfortably around them, and they, mother and son, alone, transformed, hoping that the power might not come on again too soon . . .

And then Clarisse McClellan said:

"Do you mind if I ask? How long've you worked at being a fireman?"

"Since I was twenty, ten years ago."

"Do you ever *read* any of the books you burn?"

He laughed. "That's against the law!"

"Oh. Of course."

"It's fine work. Monday burn Millay, Wednesday Whitman, Friday Faulkner, burn 'em to ashes, then burn the ashes. That's our official slogan."

They walked still farther and the girl said, "Is it true that long ago firemen put fires *out* instead of going to start them?"

"No. Houses have *always* been fireproof, take my word for it."

"Strange. I heard once that a long time ago houses used to burn by accident and they needed firemen to *stop* the flames."

He laughed.

She glanced quickly over. "Why are you laughing?"

"I don't know." He started to laugh again and stopped. "Why?"

"You laugh when I haven't been funny and you

answer right off. You never stop to think what I've asked you."

He stopped walking. "You *are* an odd one," he said, looking at her. "Haven't you any respect?"

"I don't mean to be insulting. It's just I love to watch people too much, I guess."

"Well, doesn't this mean *anything* to you?" He tapped the numerals 451 stitched on his char-colored sleeve.

"Yes," she whispered. She increased her pace. "Have you ever watched the jet cars racing on the boulevards down that way?"

"You're changing the subject!"

"I sometimes think drivers don't know what grass is, or flowers, because they never see them slowly," she said. "If you showed a driver a green blur, Oh yes! he'd say, that's grass! A pink blur? That's a rose garden! White blurs are houses. Brown blurs are cows. My uncle drove slowly on a highway once. He drove forty miles an hour and they jailed him for two days. Isn't that funny, and sad, too?"

"You think too many things," said Montag, uneasily.

"I rarely watch the 'parlor walls' or go to races or Fun Parks. So I've lots of time for crazy thoughts, I guess. Have you seen the two hundred-foot-long billboards in the country beyond town? Did you know that once billboards were only twenty feet long? But cars started rushing by so quickly they had to stretch the advertising out so it would last."

"I didn't know that!" Montag laughed abruptly.

"Bet I know something else you don't. There's dew on the grass in the morning."

He suddenly couldn't remember if he had known this or not, and it made him quite irritable.

"And if you look"—she nodded at the sky— "there's a man in the moon."

He hadn't looked for a long time.

They walked the rest of the way in silence, hers thoughtful, his a kind of clenching and uncomfortable silence in which he shot her accusing glances. When they reached her house all its lights were blazing.

"What's going on?" Montag had rarely seen that many house lights.

"Oh, just my mother and father and uncle sitting around, talking. It's like being a pedestrian, only rarer. My uncle was arrested another time—did I tell you?—for being a pedestrian. Oh, we're *most* peculiar."

"But what do you *talk* about?"

She laughed at this. "Good night!" She started up her walk. Then she seemed to remember something and came back to look at him with wonder and curiosity. "Are you happy?" she said.

"Am I *what*?" he cried.

But she was gone—running in the moonlight. Her front door shut gently.

"Happy! Of all the nonsense."

He stopped laughing.

He put his hand into the glove hole of his front door and let it know his touch. The front door slid open.

Of course I'm happy. What does she think? I'm *not*? he asked the quiet rooms. He stood looking up at the ventilator grille in the hall and suddenly remembered that something lay hidden behind the grille, something that seemed to peer down at him now. He moved his eyes quickly away.

What a strange meeting on a strange night. He remembered nothing like it save one afternoon a year ago when he had met an old man in the park and *they* had talked . . .

Montag shook his head. He looked at a blank wall. The girl's face was there, really quite beautiful in memory: astonishing, in fact. She had a very thin face like the dial of a small clock seen faintly in a dark room in the middle of a night when you waken to see the time and see the clock telling you the hour and the minute and the second, with a white silence and a glowing, all certainty and knowing what it has to tell of the night passing swiftly on toward further darknesses, but moving also toward a new sun.

"What?" asked Montag of that other self, the subconscious idiot that ran babbling at times, quite independent of will, habit, and conscience.

He glanced back at the wall. How like a mirror, too, her face. Impossible; for how many people did you know who refracted your own light to you? People were more often—he searched for a simile, found one in his work—torches, blazing away until they whiffed out. How rarely did other people's faces take of you and throw back to you your own expression, your own innermost trembling thought?

What incredible power of identification the girl had; she was like the eager watcher of a marionette show, anticipating each flicker of an eyelid, each gesture of his hand, each flick of a finger, the moment before it began. How long had they walked together? Three minutes? Five? Yet how large that time seemed

11

now. How immense a figure she was on the stage before him; what a shadow she threw on the wall with her slender body! He felt that if his eye itched, she might blink. And if the muscles of his jaws stretched imperceptibly, she would yawn long before he would.

Why, he thought, now that I think of it, she almost seemed to be waiting for me there, in the street, so damned late at night . . .

He opened the bedroom door.

It was like coming into the cold marbled room of a mausoleum after the moon has set. Complete darkness, not a hint of the silver world outside, the windows tightly shut, the chamber a tomb world where no sound from the great city could penetrate. The room was not empty.

He listened.

The little mosquito-delicate dancing hum in the air, the electrical murmur of a hidden wasp snug in its special pink warm nest. The music was almost loud enough so he could follow the tune.

He felt his smile slide away, melt, fold over and down on itself like a tallow skin, like the stuff of a fantastic candle burning too long and now collapsing and now blown out. Darkness. He was not happy. He was not happy. He said the words to himself. He recognized this as the true state of affairs. He wore his happiness like a mask and the girl had run off across the lawn with the mask and there was no way of going to knock on her door and ask for it back.

Without turning on the light he imagined how this room would look. His wife stretched on the bed, uncovered and cold, like a body displayed on the lid of a tomb, her eyes fixed to the ceiling by invisible threads of steel, immovable. And in her ears the little Seashells, the thimble radios tamped tight, and an electronic ocean of sound, of music and talk and music and talk coming in, coming in on the shore of her unsleeping mind. The room was indeed empty. Every night the waves came in and bore her off on their great tides of sound, floating her, wide-eyed, toward morning. There had been no night in the last two years that Mildred had not swum that sea, had not gladly gone down in it for the third time.

The room was cold but nonetheless he felt he could not breathe. He did not wish to open the drapes and open the French windows, for he did not want the moon to come into the room. So, with the feeling of a man who will die in the next hour for lack of air, he felt his way toward his open, separate, and therefore cold bed.

An instant before his foot hit the object on the floor he knew he would hit such an object. It was not unlike the feeling he had experienced before turning the corner and almost knocking the girl down. His foot, sending vibrations ahead, received back echoes of the small barrier across its path even as the foot swung. His foot kicked. The object gave a dull clink and slid off in darkness.

He stood very straight and listened to the person on the dark bed in the completely featureless night. The breath coming out the nostrils was so faint it stirred only the farthest fringes of life, a small leaf, a black feather, a single fibre of hair.

He still did not want outside light. He pulled out his igniter, felt the salamander etched on its silver disc, gave it a flick . . .

Two moonstones looked up at him in the light of his small hand-held fire; two pale moonstones buried in a creek of clear water over which the life of the world ran, not touching them.

"Mildred!"

Her face was like a snow-covered island upon which rain might fall, but it felt no rain; over which clouds might pass their moving shadows, but she felt no shadow. There was only the singing of the thimble-wasps in her tamped-shut ears, and her eyes all glass, and breath going in and out, softly, faintly, in and out her nostrils, and her not caring whether it came or went, went or came.

The object he had sent tumbling with his foot now glinted under the edge of his own bed. The small crystal bottle of sleeping tablets which earlier today had been filled with thirty capsules and which now lay uncapped and empty in the light of the tiny flare.

As he stood there the sky over the house screamed. There was a tremendous ripping sound as if two giant hands had torn ten thousand miles of black linen down the seam. Montag was cut in half. He felt his chest chopped down and split apart. The jet bombers going over, going over, going over, one two, one two, one two, six of them, nine of them, twelve of them, one and one and one and another and another and another, did all the screaming for him. He opened his own mouth and let their shriek come down and out between his bared teeth. The house shook. The flare went out in his hand. The moonstones vanished. He felt his hand plunge toward the telephone.

The jets were gone. He felt his lips move, brushing the mouthpiece of the phone. "Emergency hospital." A terrible whisper.

He felt that the stars had been pulverized by the sound of the black jets and that in the morning the earth would be covered with their dust like a strange snow. That was his idiot thought as he stood shivering in the dark, and let his lips go on moving and moving.

They had this machine. They had two machines, really. One of them slid down into your stomach like a black cobra down an echoing well looking for all the old water and the old time gathered there. It drank up the green matter that flowed to the top in a slow boil. Did it drink of the darkness? Did it suck out all the poisons accumulated with the years? It fed in silence with an occasional sound of inner suffocation and blind searching. It had an Eye. The impersonal operator of the machine could, by wearing a special optical helmet, gaze into the soul of the person whom he was pumping out. What did the Eye see? He did not say. He saw but did not see what the Eye saw. The entire operation was not unlike the digging of a trench in one's yard. The woman on the bed was no more than a hard stratum of marble they had reached. Go on, anyway, shove the bore down, slush up the emptiness, if such a thing could be brought out in the throb of the suction snake. The operator stood smoking a cigarette. The other machine was working, too.

The other machine, operated by an equally impersonal fellow in nonstainable reddish-brown coveralls. This machine pumped all of the blood from the body and replaced it with fresh blood and serum.

"Got to clean 'em out both ways," said the operator, standing over the silent woman. "No use getting the stomach if you don't clean the blood. Leave that stuff in the blood and the blood hits the brain like a mallet, bang, a couple thousand times and the brain just gives up, just quits."

"Stop it!" said Montag.

"I was just sayin'," said the operator.

"Are you done?" said Montag.

They shut the machines up tight. "We're done." His anger did not even touch them. They stood with the cigarette smoke curling around their noses and into their eyes without making them blink or squint. "That's fifty bucks."

"First, why don't you tell me if she'll be all right?"

"Sure, she'll be okay. We got all the mean stuff right in our suitcase here, it can't get at her now. As I said, you take out the old and put in the new and you're okay."

"Neither of you is an M. D. Why didn't they send an M. D. from Emergency?"

"Hell!" The operator's cigarette moved on his lip. "We get these cases nine or ten a night. Got so many, starting a few years ago, we had the special machines built. With the optical lens, of course, that was new; the rest is ancient. You don't need an M. D., case like this; all you need is two handymen, clean up the problem in half an hour. Look"—he started for the door—"we gotta go. Just had another call on the old ear thimble. Ten blocks from here. Someone else just jumped off the cap of a pillbox. Call if you need us again. Keep her quiet. We got a contrasedative in her. She'll wake up hungry. So long."

And the men with the cigarettes in their straight-lined mouths, the men with the eyes of puff adders, took up their load of machine and tube, their case of liquid melancholy and the slow dark sludge of nameless stuff, and strolled out the door.

Montag sank down into a chair and looked at this woman. Her eyes were closed now, gently, and he put out his hand to feel the warmness of breath on his palm.

"Mildred," he said, at last.

There are too many of us, he thought. There are billions of us and that's too many. Nobody knows anyone. Strangers come and violate you. Strangers come and cut your heart out. Strangers come and take your blood. Good God, who *were* those men? I never saw them before in my *life!*

Half an hour passed.

The bloodstream in this woman was new and it seemed to have done a new thing to her. Her cheeks were very pink and her lips were very fresh and full of color and they looked soft and relaxed. Someone else's blood there. If only someone else's flesh and brain and memory. If only they could have taken her mind along to the dry cleaner's and emptied the pockets and steamed and cleansed it and re-blocked it and brought it back in the morning. If only . . .

He got up and put back the drapes and opened the windows wide to let the night air in. It was two o'clock in the morning. Was it only an hour ago, Clarisse McClellan in the street, and him coming in, and the dark room and his foot kicking the little crystal bottle? Only an hour, but the world had melted down and sprung up in a new and colorless form.

Laughter blew across the moon-colored lawn from the house of Clarisse and her father and mother and the uncle who smiled so quietly and so earnestly. Above all, their laughter was relaxed and hearty and not forced in any way, coming from the house that was so brightly lit this late at night while all the other houses were kept to themselves in darkness. Montag heard the voices talking, talking, talking, giving, talking, weaving, reweaving their hypnotic web.

Montag moved out through the French windows and crossed the lawn, without even thinking of it. He stood outside the talking house in the shadows, thinking he might even tap on their door and whisper, "Let me come in. I won't say anything. I just want to listen. What is it you're saying?"

But instead he stood there, very cold, his face a mask of ice, listening to a man's voice (the uncle?) moving along at an easy pace:

"Well, after all, this is the age of the disposable tissue. Blow your nose on a person, wad them, flush them away, reach for another, blow, wad, flush. Everyone using everyone else's coattails. How are you supposed to root for the home team when you don't even have a program or know the names? For that matter, what color jerseys are they wearing as they trot out on the field?"

Montag moved back to his own house, left the window wide, checked Mildred, tucked the covers about her carefully, and then lay down with the moonlight on his cheekbones and on the frowning ridges in his brow, with the moonlight distilled in each eye to form a silver cataract there.

One drop of rain. Clarisse. Another drop. Mildred. A third. The uncle. A fourth. The fire tonight. One, Clarisse. Two, Mildred. Three, uncle. Four, fire.

One, Mildred, two, Clarisse. One, two, three, four,
five, Clarisse, Mildred, uncle, fire, sleeping tablets,
men disposable tissue, coattails, blow, wad, flush,
Clarisse, Mildred, uncle, fire, tablets, tissues, blow,
wad, flush. One, two, three, one, two, three! Rain.
The storm. The uncle laughing. Thunder falling downstairs. The whole world pouring down. The fire gush-
ing up in a volcano. All rushing on down around
in a spouting roar and rivering stream toward morning.

"I don't know anything any more," he said, and
let a sleep lozenge dissolve on his tongue.

At nine in the morning, Mildred's bed was empty.

Montag got up quickly, his heart pumping, and
ran down the hall and stopped at the kitchen door.

Toast popped out of the silver toaster, was seized
by a spidery metal hand that drenched it with melted
butter.

Mildred watched the toast delivered to her plate.
She had both ears plugged with electronic bees that
were humming the hour away. She looked up suddenly, saw him, and nodded.

"You all right?" he asked.

She was an expert at lip reading from ten years
of apprenticeship at Seashell ear thimbles. She
nodded again. She set the toaster clicking away at
another piece of bread.

Montag sat down.

His wife said, "I don't know *why* I should be so
hungry."

"You—"

"I'm *hungry*."

"Last night," he began.

"Didn't sleep well. Feel terrible," she said. "God, I'm hungry. I can't figure it."

"Last night—" he said again.

She watched his lips casually. "What about last night?"

"Don't you remember?"

"What? Did we have a wild party or something? Feel like I've a hangover. God, I'm hungry. Who was here?"

"A few people," he said.

"That's what I thought." She chewed her toast. "Sore stomach, but I'm hungry as all get-out. Hope I didn't do anything foolish at the party."

"No," he said, quietly.

The toaster spidered out a piece of buttered bread for him. He held it in his hand, feeling obligated.

"You don't look so hot yourself," said his wife.

In the late afternoon it rained and the entire world was dark gray. He stood in the hall of his house, putting on his badge with the orange salamander burning across it. He stood looking up at the air-conditioning vent in the hall for a long time. His wife in the TV parlor paused long enough from reading her script to glance up. "Hey," she said. "The man's *thinking!*"

"Yes," he said. "I wanted to talk to you." He paused. "You took all the pills in your bottle last night."

"Oh, I wouldn't do that," she said, surprised.

"The bottle was empty."

"I wouldn't do a thing like that. Why would I do a thing like that?" she said.

"Maybe you took two pills and forgot and took two more, and forgot again and took two more, and were so dopey you kept right on until you had thirty or forty of them in you."

"Heck," she said, "what would I want to go and do a silly thing like that for?"

"I don't know," he said.

She was quite obviously waiting for him to go. "I didn't do that," she said. "Never in a billion years."

"All right, if you say so," he said.

"That's what the lady said." She turned back to her script.

"What's on this afternoon?" he asked, tiredly.

She didn't look up from the script again. "Well, this is a play comes on the wall-to-wall circuit in ten minutes. They mailed me my part this morning. I sent in some boxtops. They write the script with one part missing. It's a new idea. The homemaker, that's me, is the missing part. When it comes time for the missing lines, they all look at me out of the three walls and I say the lines. Here, for instance, the man says, 'What do you think of this whole idea, Helen?' And he looks at me sitting here center stage, see? And I say, I say—" She paused and ran her finger under a line on the script. " 'I think that's fine!' And then they go on with the play until he says, 'Do you agree to that, Helen?' and I say, 'I sure do!' Isn't that fun, Guy?"

He stood in the hall, looking at her.

"It's sure fun," she said.

"What's the play about?"

"I just told you. There are these people named Bob and Ruth and Helen."

"Oh."

"It's really fun. It'll be even more fun when we can afford to have the fourth wall installed. How long you figure before we save up and get the fourth wall torn out and a fourth wall-TV put in? It's only two thousand dollars."

"That's one-third of my yearly pay."

"It's only two thousand dollars," she replied. "And I should think you'd consider me sometimes. If we had a fourth wall, why it'd be just like this room wasn't ours at all, but all kinds of exotic people's rooms. We could do without a few things."

"We're already doing without a few things to pay for the third wall. It was put in only two months ago, remember?"

"Is that all it was?" She sat looking at him for a long moment. "Well, good-bye, dear."

"Good-bye," he said. He stopped and turned around. "Does it have a happy ending?"

"I haven't read that far."

He walked over, read the last page, nodded, folded the script, and handed it back to her. He walked out of the house into the rain.

The rain was thinning away and the girl was walking in the center of the sidewalk with her head up and the few drops falling on her face. She smiled when she saw Montag.

"Hello!"

He said hello and then said, "What are you up to now?"

"I'm still crazy. The rain feels good. I love to walk in it."

"I don't think I'd like that," he said.

"You might if you tried."

"I never have."

She licked her lips. "Rain even tastes good."

"What do you do, go around trying everything once?" he asked.

"Sometimes twice." She looked at something in her hand.

"What've you got there?" he said.

"I guess it's the last of the dandelions this year. I didn't think I'd find one on the lawn this late. Have you ever heard of rubbing it under your chin? Look." She touched her chin with the flower, laughing.

"Why?"

"If it rubs off, it means I'm in love. Has it?"

He could hardly do anything else but look.

"Well?" she said.

"You're yellow under there."

"Fine! Let's try *you* now."

"It won't work for me."

"Here." Before he could move she had put the dandelion under his chin. He drew back and she laughed. "Hold still!"

She peered under his chin and frowned.

"Well?" he said.

"What a shame," she said. "You're not in love with anyone."

"Yes, I am!"

"It doesn't show."

"I am, very much in love!" He tried to conjure up a face to fit the words, but there was no face. "I am!"

"Oh, please don't look that way."

"It's that dandelion," he said. "You've used it all up on yourself. That's why it won't work for me."

"Of course, that must be it. Oh, now I've upset you, I can see I have; I'm sorry, really I am." She touched his elbow.

"No, no," he said, quickly, "I'm all right."

"I've got to be going, so say you forgive me. I don't want you angry with me."

"I'm not angry. Upset, yes."

"I've got to go see my psychiatrist now. They *make* me go. I make up things to say. I don't know what he thinks of me. He says I'm a regular onion! I keep him busy peeling away the layers."

"I'm inclined to believe you need the psychiatrist," said Montag.

"You don't mean that."

He took a breath and let it out and at last said, "No, I don't mean that."

"The psychiatrist wants to know why I go out and hike around in the forests and watch the birds and collect butterflies. I'll show you my collection some-day."

"Good."

"They want to know what I do with all my time. I tell them that sometimes I just sit and *think*. But I won't tell them what. I've got them running. And sometimes, I tell them, I like to put my head back, like this, and let the rain fall in my mouth. It tastes just like wine. Have you ever tried it?"

"No, I—"

"You *have* forgiven me, haven't you?"

"Yes." He thought about it. "Yes, I have. God knows why. You're peculiar, you're aggravating, yet you're easy to forgive. You say you're seventeen?"

"Well—next month."

"How odd. How strange. And my wife thirty and

yet you seem so much older at times. I can't get over it."

"You're peculiar yourself, Mr. Montag. Sometimes I even forget you're a fireman. Now, may I make you angry again?"

"Go ahead."

"How did it start? How did you get into it? How did you pick your work and how did you happen to think to take the job you have? You're not like the others. I've seen a few; I *know*. When I talk, you look at me. When I said something about the moon, you looked at the moon, last night. The others would never do that. The others would walk off and leave me talking. Or threaten me. No one has time any more for anyone else. You're one of the few who put up with me. That's why I think it's so strange you're a fireman. It just doesn't seem right for you, somehow."

He felt his body divide itself into a hotness and a coldness, a softness and a hardness, a trembling and a not trembling, the two halves grinding one upon the other.

"You'd better run on to your appointment," he said.

And she ran off and left him standing there in the rain. Only after a long time did he move.

And then, very slowly, as he walked, he tilted his head back in the rain, for just a few moments, and opened his mouth . . .

The Mechanical Hound slept but did not sleep, lived but did not live in its gently humming, gently vibrating, softly illuminated kennel back in a dark corner of the firehouse. The dim light of one in the morning, the moonlight from the open sky framed through the great window, touched here and there on the brass and the copper and the steel of the faintly trembling beast. Light flickered on bits of ruby glass and on sensitive capillary hairs in the nylon-brushed nostrils of the creature that quivered gently, gently, its eight legs spidered under it on rubber-padded paws.

Montag slid down the brass pole. He went out to look at the city and the clouds had cleared away completely, and he lit a cigarette and came back to bend down and look at the Hound. It was like a great bee come home from some field where the honey is full of poison wildness, of insanity and nightmare, its body crammed with that overrich nectar, and now it was sleeping the evil out of itself.

"Hello," whispered Montag, fascinated as always with the dead beast, the living beast.

Nights when things got dull, which was every night, the men slid down the brass poles and set the ticking combinations of the olfactory system of the Hound and let loose rats in the firehouse areaway, and sometimes chickens, and sometimes cats that would have to be drowned anyway, and there would be betting to see which of the cats or chickens or rats the Hound would seize first. The animals were turned loose. Three seconds later the game was done, the rat, cat, or chicken caught half across the areaway, gripped in gentling paws while a four-inch hollow steel needle plunged down from the proboscis of the Hound to inject massive jolts of morphine or procaine. The pawn was then tossed in the incinerator. A new game began.

Montag stayed upstairs most nights when this

went on. There had been a time two years ago when he had bet with the best of them, and lost a week's salary and faced Mildred's insane anger, which showed itself in veins and blotches. But now nights he lay in his bunk, face turned to the wall, listening to the whoops of laughter below and the piano-string scurry of rat feet, the violin squeaking of mice, and the great shadowing, motioned silence of the Hound leaping out like a moth in the raw light, finding, holding its victim, inserting the needle and going back to its kennel to die as if a switch had been turned.

Montag touched the muzzle.

The Hound growled.

Montag jumped back.

The Hound half rose in its kennel and looked at him with green-blue neon light flickering in its suddenly activated eye-bulbs. It growled again, a strange rasping combination of electrical sizzle, a frying sound, a scraping of metal, a turning of cogs that seemed rusty and ancient with suspicion.

"No, no, boy," said Montag, his heart pounding.

He saw the silver needle extend upon the air an inch, pull back, extend, pull back. The growl simmered in the beast and it looked at him.

Montag backed up. The Hound took a step from its kennel. Montag grabbed the brass pole with one hand. The pole, reacting, slid upward and took him through the ceiling, quietly. He stepped off in the half-lit deck of the upper level. He was trembling and his face was green-white. Below, the Hound had sunk back down upon its eight incredible insect legs and was humming to itself again, its multi-faceted eyes at peace.

Montag stood, letting the fears pass, by the drophole. Behind him, four men at a card table under a green-lidded light in the corner glanced briefly but said nothing. Only the man with the Captain's hat and the sign of the phoenix on his hat, at last, curious, his playing cards in his thin hand, talked across the long room.

"Montag? . . ."

"It doesn't *like* me," said Montag.

"What, the Hound?" The Captain studied his cards. "Come off it. It doesn't like or dislike. It just 'functions.' It's like a lesson in ballistics. It has a trajectory we decide on for it. It follows through. It targets itself, homes itself, and cuts off. It's only copper wire, storage batteries, and electricity."

Montag swallowed. "Its calculators can be set to any combination, so many amino acids, so much sulphur, so much butterfat and alkaline. Right?"

"We all know that."

"All of those chemical balances and percentages on all of us here in the House are recorded in the master file downstairs. It would be easy for someone to set up a partial combination on the Hound's 'memory,' a touch of amino acids, perhaps. That would account for what the animal did just now. Reacted toward me."

"Hell," said the Captain.

"Irritated, but not completely angry. Just enough 'memory' set up in it by someone so it growled when I touched it."

"Who would do a thing like that?" asked the Captain. "You haven't any enemies here, Guy."

"None that I know of."

"We'll have the Hound checked by our technicians tomorrow."

"This isn't the first time it's threatened me," said Montag. "Last month it happened twice."

"We'll fix it up. Don't worry."

But Montag did not move and only stood thinking of the ventilator grille in the hall at home and what lay hidden behind the grille. If someone here in the firehouse knew about the ventilator then mightn't they "tell" the Hound? . . .

The Captain came over to the drophole and gave Montag a questioning glance.

"I was just figuring," said Montag, "what does the Hound think about down there nights? Is it coming alive on us, really? It makes me cold."

"It doesn't think anything we don't want it to think."

"That's sad," said Montag, quietly, "because all we put into it is hunting and finding and killing. What a shame if that's all it can ever know."

Beatty snorted, gently. "Hell! It's a fine bit of craftsmanship, a good rifle that can fetch its own target and guarantees the bull's-eye every time."

"That's why," said Montag, "I wouldn't want to be its next victim."

"Why? You got a guilty conscience about something?"

Montag glanced up swiftly.

Beatty stood there looking at him steadily with his eyes, while his mouth opened and began to laugh, very softly.

One two three four five six seven days. And as many times he came out of the house and Clarisse was there somewhere in the world. Once he saw her shaking a walnut tree, once he saw her sitting on the lawn knitting a blue sweater, three or four times he found a bouquet of late flowers on his porch, or a handful of chestnuts in a little sack, or some autumn leaves neatly pinned to a sheet of white paper and thumbtacked to his door. Every day Clarisse walked him to the corner. One day it was raining, the next it was clear, the day after that the wind blew strong, and the day after that it was mild and calm, and the day after that calm day was a day like the furnace of summer and Clarisse with her face all sunburnt by late afternoon.

"Why is it," he said, one time, at the subway entrance, "I feel I've known you so many years?"

"Because I like you," she said, "and I don't want anything from you. And because we know each other."

"You make me feel very old and very much like a father."

"Now you explain," she said, "why you haven't any daughters like me, if you love children so much?"

"I don't know."

"You're joking!"

"I mean—" He stopped and shook his head. "Well, my wife, she . . . she just never wanted any children at all."

The girl stopped smiling. "I'm sorry. I really thought you were having fun at my expense. I'm a fool."

"No, no," he said. "It was a good question. It's been a long time since anyone cared enough to ask. A good question."

"Let's talk about something else. Have you ever smelled old leaves? Don't they smell like cinnamon? Here. Smell."

"Why, yes, it *is* like cinnamon in a way."

She looked at him with her clear dark eyes. "You always seem shocked."

"It's just I haven't had time—"

"Did you look at the stretched-out billboards like I told you?"

"I think so. Yes." He had to laugh.

"Your laugh sounds much nicer than it did."

"Does it?"

"Much more relaxed."

He felt at ease and comfortable. "Why aren't you in school? I see you every day wandering around."

"Oh, they don't miss me," she said. "I'm anti-social, they say. I don't mix. It's so strange. I'm very social indeed. It all depends on what you mean by social, doesn't it? Social to me means talking to you about things like this." She rattled some chestnuts that had fallen off the tree in the front yard. "Or talking about how strange the world is. Being with people is nice. But I don't think it's social to get a bunch of people together and then not let them talk, do you? An hour of TV class, an hour of basketball or baseball or running, another hour of transcription history or painting pictures, and more sports, but do you know, we never ask questions, or at least most don't; they just run the answers at you, bing, bing, bing, and us sitting there for four more hours of film teacher. That's not social to me at all. It's a lot of funnels and a lot of water poured down the spout and out the bottom, and them telling us it's wine when it's not. They run us so ragged by the end of the day we can't do anything but go to bed or head for a Fun Park to bully people around, break windowpanes in the Window Smasher place or wreck cars in the Car Wrecker place with the big steel ball. Or go out in the cars and race on the streets, trying to see how close you can get to lampposts, playing 'chicken' and 'knock hubcaps.' I guess I'm everything they say I am, all right. I haven't any friends. That's supposed to prove I'm abnormal. But everyone I know is either shouting or dancing around like wild or beating up one another. Do you notice how people hurt each other nowadays?"

"You sound so very old."

"Sometimes I'm ancient. I'm afraid of children my own age. They kill each other. Did it always use to be that way? My uncle says no. Six of my friends have been shot in the last year alone. Ten of them died in car wrecks. I'm afraid of them and they don't like me because I'm afraid. My uncle says his grandfather remembered when children didn't kill each other. But that was a long time ago when they had things different. They believed in responsibility, my uncle says. Do you know, I'm responsible. I was spanked when I needed it, years ago. And I do all the shopping and housecleaning by hand.

"But most of all," she said, "I like to watch people. Sometimes I ride the subway all day and look at them and listen to them. I just want to figure out who they are and what they want and where they're going. Sometimes I even go to the Fun Parks and ride in the jet cars when they race on the edge of town at midnight and the police don't care as long as they're insured. As long as everyone has ten thousand insurance everyone's happy. Sometimes I sneak around and listen in subways. Or I listen at soda fountains, and do you know what?"

"What?"

"People don't talk about anything."

"Oh, they *must!*"

"No, not anything. They name a lot of cars or clothes or swimming pools mostly and say how swell! But they all say the same things and nobody says anything different from anyone else. And most of the time in the cafes they have the joke boxes on and the same jokes most of the time, or the musical wall lit and all the colored patterns running up and down, but it's only color and all abstract. And at the museums, have you *ever* been? *All* abstract. That's all there is now. My uncle says it was different once. A long time back sometimes pictures said things or even showed *people*."

"Your uncle said, your uncle said. Your uncle must be a remarkable man."

"He is. He certainly is. Well, I got to be going. Good-bye, Mr. Montag."

"Good-bye."

"Good-bye . . ."

One two three four five six seven days: the firehouse.

"Montag, you shin that pole like a bird up a tree."

Third day.

"Montag, I see you came in the back door this time. The Hound bother you?"

"No, no."

Fourth day.

"Montag, a funny thing. Heard tell this morning. Fireman in Seattle purposely set a Mechanical Hound to his own chemical complex and let it loose. What kind of suicide would you call *that?*"

Five, six, seven days.

And then, Clarisse was gone. He didn't know what there was about the afternoon, but it was not seeing her somewhere in the world. The lawn was empty, the trees empty, the street empty, and while at first he did not even know he missed her or was even looking for her, the fact was that by the time he reached the subway, there were vague stirrings of dis-ease in him. Something was the matter, his routine had been disturbed. A simple routine, true, established in a short few days, and yet? . . . He almost turned back to make the walk again, to give her time to appear. He was certain if he tried the same route, everything would work out fine. But it was late, and the arrival of his train put a stop to his plan.

The flutter of cards, motion of hands, of eyelids, the drone of the time-voice in the firehouse ceiling ". . . one thirty-five, Thursday morning, November fourth . . . one thirty-six . . . one thirty-seven A.M. . . ." The tick of the playing cards on the greasy tabletop, all the sounds came to Montag, behind his closed eyes, behind the barrier he had momentarily erected. He could feel the firehouse full of glitter and shine and silence, of brass colors, the colors of coins, of gold, of silver. The unseen men across the table were sighing on their cards, waiting. ". . . one forty-five . . ." The voice clock mourned out the cold hour of a cold morning of a still colder year.

"What's wrong, Montag?"

Montag opened his eyes.

A radio hummed somewhere. ". . . war may be

declared any hour. This country stands ready to defend its . . ."

The firehouse trembled as a great flight of jet planes whistled a single note across the black morning sky.

Montag blinked. Beatty was looking at him as if he were a museum statue. At any moment, Beatty might rise and walk about him, touching, exploring his guilt and self-consciousness. Guilt? What guilt was that?

"Your play, Montag."

Montag looked at these men whose faces were sunburnt by a thousand real and ten thousand imaginary fires, whose work flushed their cheeks and fevered their eyes. These men who looked steadily into their platinum igniter flames as they lit their eternally burning black pipes. They and their charcoal hair and soot-colored brows and bluish-ash-smeared cheeks where they had shaven close; but their heritage showed. Montag started up, his mouth opened. Had he ever seen a fireman that *didn't* have black hair, black brows, a fiery face, and a blue-steel shaved but unshaved look? These men were all mirror images of himself! Were all firemen picked then for their looks as well as their proclivities? The color of cinders and ash about them, and the continual smell of burning from their pipes. Captain Beatty there, rising in thunderheads of tobacco smoke. Beatty opening a fresh tobacco packet, crumpling the cellophane into a sound of fire.

Montag looked at the cards in his own hands. "I—I've been thinking. About the fire last week. About the man whose library we fixed. What happened to him?"

35

"They took him screaming off to the asylum."

"He wasn't insane."

Beatty arranged his cards quietly. "Any man's insane who thinks he can fool the government and us."

"I've tried to imagine," said Montag, "just how it would feel. I mean, to have firemen burn *our* houses and *our* books."

"We haven't any books."

"But if we did have some."

"You *got* some?"

Beatty blinked slowly.

"No." Montag gazed beyond them to the wall with the typed lists of a million forbidden books. Their names leapt in fire, burning down the years under his ax and his hose which sprayed not water but kerosene. "No." But in his mind, a cool wind started up and blew out of the ventilator grille at home, softly, softly, chilling his face. And, again, he saw himself in a green park talking to an old man, a very old man, and the wind from the park was cold, too.

Montag hesitated. "Was—was it always like this? The firehouse, our work? I mean, well, once upon a time . . ."

"Once upon a time!" Beatty said. "What kind of talk is *that?*"

Fool, thought Montag to himself, you'll give it away. At the last fire, a book of fairy tales, he'd glanced at a single line. "I mean," he said, "in the old days, before homes were completely fire-proofed—" Suddenly it seemed a much younger voice was speaking for him. He opened his mouth and it was Clarisse McClellan saying, "Didn't firemen *prevent* fires rather than stoke them up and get them going?"

"That's rich!" Stoneman and Black drew forth their rule books, which also contained brief histories of the Firemen of America, and laid them out where Montag, though long familiar with them, might read:

Established, 1790, to burn English-influenced books in the Colonies. First Fireman: Benjamin Franklin.

RULE 1. Answer the alarm swiftly.
     2. Start the fire swiftly.
     3. Burn everything.
     4. Report back to firehouse immediately.
     5. Stand alert for other alarms.

Everyone watched Montag. He did not move.

The alarm sounded.

The bell in the ceiling kicked itself two hundred times. Suddenly there were four empty chairs. The cards fell in a flurry of snow. The brass pole shivered. The men were gone.

Montag sat in his chair. Below, the orange dragon coughed to life.

Montag slid down the pole like a man in a dream.

The Mechanical Hound leapt up in its kennel, its eyes all green flame.

"Montag, you forgot your helmet!"

He seized it off the wall behind him, ran, leapt, and they were off, the night wind hammering about their siren scream and their mighty metal thunder!

It was a flaking three-story house in the ancient part of the city, a century old if it was a day, but

like all houses it had been given a thin fireproof
plastic sheath many years ago, and this preservative
shell seemed to be the only thing holding it in the
sky.

"Here we are!"

The engine slammed to a stop. Beatty, Stoneman,
and Black ran up the sidewalk, suddenly odious and
fat in their plump fireproof slickers. Montag followed.

They crashed the front door and grabbed at a
woman, though she was not running, she was not
trying to escape. She was only standing, weaving
from side to side, her eyes fixed upon a nothingness
in the wall, as if they had struck her a terrible blow
upon the head. Her tongue was moving in her mouth,
and her eyes seemed to be trying to remember something and then they remembered and her tongue
moved again:

" 'Play the man, Master Ridley; we shall this
day light such a candle, by God's grace, in England,
as I trust shall never be put out.' "

"Enough of that!" said Beatty. "Where are they?"

He slapped her face with amazing objectivity and
repeated the question. The old woman's eyes came to
a focus upon Beatty. "You know where they are or
you wouldn't be here," she said.

Stoneman held out the telephone alarm card with
the complaint signed in telephone duplicate on the
back:

Have reason to suspect attic; 11 No. Elm, City.
                                              E. B.

"That would be Mrs. Blake, my neighbor," said
the woman, reading the initials.

"All right, men, let's get 'em!"

Next thing they were up in musty blackness swinging silver hatchets at doors that were, after all, unlocked, tumbling through like boys all rollick and shout. "Hey!" A fountain of books sprang down upon Montag as he climbed shuddering up the sheer stairwell. How inconvenient! Always before it had been like snuffing a candle. The police went first and adhesive-taped the victim's mouth and bandaged him off into their glittering beetle cars, so when you arrived you found an empty house. You weren't hurting anyone, you were hurting only *things!* And since things really couldn't be hurt, since things felt nothing, and things don't scream or whimper, as this woman might begin to scream and cry out, there was nothing to tease your conscience later. You were simply cleaning up. Janitorial work, essentially. Everything to its proper place. Quick with the kerosene! Who's got a match!

But now, tonight, someone had slipped. This woman was spoiling the ritual. The men were making too much noise, laughing, joking, to cover her terrible accusing silence below. She made the empty rooms roar with accusation and shake down a fine dust of guilt that was sucked in their nostrils as they plunged about. It was neither cricket nor correct. Montag felt an immense irritation. She shouldn't be here, on top of everything!

Books bombarded his shoulders, his arms, his upturned face. A book lit, almost obediently, like a white pigeon, in his hands, wings fluttering. In the dim, wavering light, a page hung open and it was like a snowy feather, the words delicately painted thereon. In all the rush and fervor, Montag had only an instant to read a line, but it blazed in his mind for the next minute as if stamped there with fiery steel. "Time has fallen asleep in the afternoon sunshine." He dropped the book. Immediately, another fell into his arms.

"Montag, up here!"

Montag's hand closed like a mouth, crushed the book with wild devotion, with an insanity of mindlessness to his chest. The men above were hurling shovelfuls of magazines into the dusty air. They fell like slaughtered birds and the woman stood below, like a small girl, among the bodies.

Montag had done nothing. His hand had done it all, his hand, with a brain of its own, with a conscience and a curiosity in each trembling finger, had turned thief. Now it plunged the book back under his arm, pressed it tight to sweating armpit, rushed out empty, with a magician's flourish! Look here! Innocent! Look!

He gazed, shaken, at that white hand. He held it way out, as if he were farsighted. He held it close, as if he were blind.

"Montag!"

He jerked about.

"Don't stand there, idiot!"

The books lay like great mounds of fishes left to dry. The men danced and slipped and fell over them. Titles glittered their golden eyes, falling, gone.

"Kerosene!"

They pumped the cold fluid from the numeraled 451 tanks strapped to their shoulders. They coated each book, they pumped rooms full of it.

They hurried downstairs, Montag staggering after them in the kerosene fumes.

"Come on, woman!"

The woman knelt among the books, touching the drenched leather and cardboard, reading the gilt titles with her fingers while her eyes accused Montag.

"You can't ever have my books," she said.

"You know the law," said Beatty. "Where's your common sense? None of those books agree with each other. You've been locked up here for years with a regular damned Tower of Babel. Snap out of it! The people in those books never lived. Come on now!"

She shook her head.

"The whole house is going up," said Beatty.

The men walked clumsily to the door. They glanced back at Montag, who stood near the woman.

"You're not leaving her here?" he protested.

"She won't come."

"Force her, then!"

Beatty raised his hand in which was concealed the igniter. "We're due back at the House. Besides, these fanatics always try suicide; the pattern's familiar."

Montag placed his hand on the woman's elbow. "You can come with me."

"No," she said. "Thank you, anyway."

"I'm counting to ten," said Beatty. "One. Two."

"Please," said Montag.

"Go on," said the woman.

"Three. Four."

"Here." Montag pulled at the woman.

The woman replied quietly, "I want to stay here."

"Five. Six."

"You can stop counting," she said. She opened the fingers of one hand slightly and in the palm of the hand was a single slender object.

An ordinary kitchen match.

The sight of it rushed the men out and down away from the house. Captain Beatty, keeping his dignity, backed slowly through the front door, his pink face burnt and shiny from a thousand fires and night excitements. God, thought Montag, how true! Always at night the alarm comes. Never by day! Is it because fire is prettier by night? More spectacle, a better show? The pink face of Beatty now showed the faintest panic in the door. The woman's hand twitched on the single matchstick. The fumes of kerosene bloomed up about her. Montag felt the hidden book pound like a heart against his chest.

"Go on," said the woman, and Montag felt himself back away and away out the door, after Beatty, down the steps, across the lawn, where the path of kerosene lay like the track of some evil snail.

On the front porch where she had come to weigh them quietly with her eyes, her quietness a condemnation, the woman stood motionless.

Beatty flicked his fingers to spark the kerosene.

He was too late. Montag gasped.

The woman on the porch reached out with contempt to them all and struck the kitchen match against the railing.

People ran out of houses all down the street.

They said nothing on their way back to the firehouse. Nobody looked at anyone else. Montag sat in the front seat with Beatty and Black. They did not even smoke their pipes. They sat there looking out the front of the great Salamander as they turned a corner and went silently on.

"Master Ridley," said Montag, at last.

"What?" said Beatty.

"She said, 'Master Ridley.' She said some crazy thing when we came in the door. 'Play the man,' she said, 'Master Ridley.' Something, something, something."

" 'We shall this day light such a candle, by God's grace, in England, as I trust shall never be put out,' " said Beatty. Stoneman glanced over at the Captain, as did Montag, startled.

Beatty rubbed his chin. "A man named Latimer said that to a man named Nicholas Ridley, as they were being burnt alive at Oxford, for heresy, on October 16, 1555."

Montag and Stoneman went back to looking at the street as it moved under the engine wheels.

"I'm full of bits and pieces," said Beatty. "Most fire captains have to be. Sometimes I surprise myself. *Watch* it, Stoneman!"

Stoneman braked the truck.

"Damn!" said Beatty. "You've gone right by the corner where we turn for the firehouse."

"Who is it?"

"Who would it be?" said Montag, leaning back against the closed door in the dark.

His wife said, at last, "Well, put on the light."

"I don't want the light."

"Come to bed."

He heard her roll impatiently; the bedsprings squealed.

"Are you drunk?" she said.

So it was the hand that started it all. He felt one hand and then the other work his coat free and let it slump to the floor. He held his pants out into an abyss and let them fall into darkness. His hands had been infected, and soon it would be his arms. He could feel the poison working up his wrists and into his elbows and his shoulders, and then the jumpover from shoulder blade to shoulder blade like a spark leaping a gap. His hands were ravenous. And his eyes were beginning to feel hunger, as if they must look at something, anything, everything.

His wife said, "What *are* you doing?"

He balanced in space with the book in his sweating cold fingers.

A minute later she said, "Well, just don't stand there in the middle of the floor."

He made a small sound.

"What?" she asked.

He made more soft sounds. He stumbled toward the bed and shoved the book clumsily under the cold pillow. He fell into bed and his wife cried out, startled. He lay far across the room from her, on a winter island separated by an empty sea. She talked to him for what seemed a long while and she talked about this and she talked about that and it was only words, like the words he had heard once in a nursery at a friend's house, a two-year-old child building word patterns, talking jargon, making pretty sounds in the air. But Montag said nothing and after a long while when he only made the small sounds, he felt her move in the room and come to his bed and stand over him and put her hand down to feel his cheek. He knew that when she pulled her hand away from his face it was wet.

Late in the night he looked over at Mildred. She was awake. There was a tiny dance of melody in the air, her Seashell was tamped in her ear again, and she was listening to far people in far places, her eyes wide and staring at the fathoms of blackness above her in the ceiling.

Wasn't there an old joke about the wife who talked so much on the telephone that her desperate husband ran out to the nearest store and telephoned her to ask what was for dinner? Well, then, why didn't he buy himself an audio-Seashell broadcasting station and talk to his wife late at night, murmur, whisper, shout, scream, yell? But what would he whisper, what would he yell? What could he say?

And suddenly she was so strange he couldn't believe he knew her at all. He was in someone else's house, like those other jokes people told of the gentleman, drunk, coming home late late at night, unlocking the wrong door, entering a wrong room, and bedding with a stranger and getting up early and going to work and neither of them the wiser.

"Millie? . . ." he whispered.

"What?"

"I didn't mean to startle you. What I want to know is . . ."

"Well?"

"When did we meet? And *where?*"

"When did we meet for *what?*" she asked.

"I mean—originally."

He knew she must be frowning in the dark.

He clarified it. "The first time we ever met, where was it, and when?"

"Why, it was at—"

She stopped.

"I don't know," she said.

He was cold. "Can't you remember?"

"It's been so long."

"Only ten years, that's all, only ten!"

"Don't get excited, I'm trying to think." She laughed an odd little laugh that went up and up. "Funny, how funny, not to remember where or when you met your husband'r wife."

He lay massaging his eyes, his brow, and the back of his neck, slowly. He held both hands over his eyes and applied a steady pressure there as if to crush memory into place. It was suddenly more important than any other thing in a lifetime that he know where he had met Mildred.

"It doesn't matter." She was up, in the bathroom now, and he heard the water running, and the swallowing sound she made.

"No, I guess not," he said.

He tried to count how many times she swallowed and he thought of the visit from the two zinc-oxide-faced men with the cigarettes in their straight-lined mouths and the Electronic-Eyed Snake winding down into the layer upon layer of night and stone and stagnant spring water, and he wanted to call out to her, how many have you taken *tonight!* the capsules! how many will you take later and not know? and so on, every hour! or maybe not tonight, tomorrow night! And me not sleeping tonight or tomorrow night or any night for a long while, now that this has started. And he thought of her lying on the bed with the two technicians standing straight over her, not bent with concern, but only standing straight, arms folded. And he remembered thinking then that if she died, he was certain he wouldn't cry. For it would be the dying of an unknown, a street face, a newspaper image, and it was suddenly so very wrong that he had begun to cry, not at death but at the thought of *not crying* at death, a silly empty man near a silly empty woman, while the hungry snake made her still more empty.

How do you get so empty? he wondered. Who takes it out of you? And that awful flower the other day, the dandelion! It had summed up everything, hadn't it? "What a shame! You're not in love with anyone!" And why not?

Well, wasn't there a wall between him and Mildred, when you came down to it? Literally not just one wall but, so far, three! And expensive, too! And the uncles, the aunts, the cousins, the nieces, the nephews, that lived in those walls, the gibbering pack of tree apes that said nothing, nothing, nothing and said it loud, loud, loud. He had taken to calling them relatives from the very first. "How's Uncle Louis today?" "Who?" "And Aunt Maude?" The most significant memory he had of Mildred, really, was of a little girl in a forest without trees (how odd!) or rather a little girl lost on a plateau where there used to be trees (you could feel the memory of their shapes all about) sitting in the center of the "living room." The living room; what a good job of labeling that was now. No matter when he came in, the walls were always talking to Mildred.

"Something must be done!"

"Yes, something must be *done!*"

"Well, let's not stand and talk!"

"Let's *do* it!"

"I'm so mad I could *spit!*"

What was it all about? Mildred couldn't say. Who was mad at whom? Mildred didn't quite know. What were they going to do? Well, said Mildred, wait around and see.

47

He had waited around to see.

A great thunderstorm of sound gushed from the walls. Music bombarded him at such an immense volume that his bones were almost shaken from their tendons; he felt his jaw vibrate, his eyes wobble in his head. He was a victim of concussion. When it was all over he felt like a man who had been thrown from a cliff, whirled in a centrifuge, and spat out over a waterfall that fell and fell into emptiness and emptiness and never—quite—touched—bottom— never—never—quite—no not quite—touched—bottom . . . and you fell so fast you didn't touch the sides either . . . never . . . quite . . . touched . . . anything.

The thunder faded. The music died.

"There," said Mildred.

And it was indeed remarkable. Something had happened. Even though the people in the walls of the room had barely moved, and nothing had really been settled, you had the impression that someone had turned on a washing machine or sucked you up in a gigantic vacuum. You drowned in music and pure cacophony. He came out of the room sweating and on the point of collapse. Behind him, Mildred sat in her chair and the voice went on again:

"Well, everything will be all right now," said an "aunt."

"Oh, don't be too sure," said a "cousin."

"Now, don't get angry!"

"Who's angry?"

"*You* are!"

"*I* am?"

"You're mad!"

"Why would I be mad!"

"Because!"

"That's all very well," cried Montag, "but what are they mad about? Who *are* these people? Who's that man and who's that woman? Are they husband and wife, are they divorced, engaged, what? Good God, *nothing's* connected up."

"They—" said Mildred. "Well, they—they had this fight, you see. They certainly fight a lot. You should listen. I think they're married. Yes, they're married. Why?"

And if it was not the three walls soon to be four walls and the dream complete, then it was the open car and Mildred driving a hundred miles an hour across town, he shouting at her and she shouting back and both trying to hear what was said, but hearing only the scream of the car. "At least keep it down to the minimum!" he yelled. "What?" she cried. "Keep it down to fifty-five, the minimum!" he shouted. "The what?" she shrieked. "Speed!" he shouted. And she pushed it up to one hundred and five miles an hour and tore the breath from his mouth.

When they stepped out of the car, she had the Seashells stuffed in her ears.

Silence. Only the wind blowing softly.

"Mildred." He stirred in bed.

He reached over and pulled the tiny musical insect out of her ear. "Mildred. Mildred?"

"Yes." Her voice was faint.

He felt he was one of the creatures electronically inserted between the slots of the phono-color walls, speaking, but the speech not piercing the crystal barrier. He could only pantomime, hoping she would turn his way and see him. They could not touch through the glass.

"Mildred, do you know that girl I was telling you about?"

"What girl?" She was almost asleep.

"The girl next door."

"What girl next door?"

"You know, the high-school girl. Clarisse, her name is."

"Oh, yes," said his wife.

"I haven't seen her for a few days—four days to be exact. Have you seen her?"

"No."

"I've meant to talk to you about her. Strange."

"Oh, I know the one you mean."

"I thought you would."

"Her," said Mildred in the dark room.

"What about her?" asked Montag.

"I meant to tell you. Forgot. Forgot."

"Tell me now. What is it?"

"I think she's gone."

"Gone?"

"Whole family moved out somewhere. But she's gone for good. I think she's dead."

"We couldn't be talking about the same girl."

"No. The same girl. McClellan. McClellan. Run over by a car. Four days ago. I'm not sure. But I think she's dead. The family moved out anyway. I don't know. But I think she's dead."

"You're not sure of it!"

"No, not sure. Pretty sure."

"Why didn't you tell me sooner?"

"Forgot."

"Four days ago!"

"I forgot all about it."

"Four days ago," he said, quietly, lying there.

They lay there in the dark room not moving, either of them. "Good night," she said.

He heard a faint rustle. Her hand moved. The electric thimble moved like a praying mantis on the pillow, touched by her hand. Now it was in her ear again, humming.

He listened and his wife was singing under her breath.

Outside the house, a shadow moved, an autumn wind rose up and faded away. But there was something else in the silence that he heard. It was like a breath exhaled upon the window. It was like a faint drift of greenish luminescent smoke, the motion of a single huge October leaf blowing across the lawn and away.

The Hound, he thought. It's out there tonight. It's out there now. If I opened the window . . .

He did not open the window.

He had chills and fever in the morning.

"You can't be sick," said Mildred.

He closed his eyes over the hotness. "Yes."

"But you were all right last night."

"No, I wasn't all right." He heard the "relatives" shouting in the parlor.

Mildred stood over his bed, curiously. He felt her there, he saw her without opening his eyes, her hair burnt by chemicals to a brittle straw, her eyes with a kind of cataract unseen but suspect far behind the pupils, the reddened pouting lips, the body as thin as a praying mantis from dieting, and her flesh like

51

white bacon. He could remember her no other way.

"Will you bring me aspirin and water?"

"You've got to get up," she said. "It's noon. You've slept five hours later than usual."

"Will you turn the parlor off?" he asked.

"That's my family."

"Will you turn it off for a sick man?"

"I'll turn it down."

She went out of the room and did nothing to the parlor and came back. "Is that better?"

"Thanks."

"That's my favorite program," she said.

"What about the aspirin?"

"You've never been sick before." She went away again.

"Well, I'm sick now. I'm not going to work tonight. Call Beatty for me."

"You acted funny last night." She returned, humming.

"Where's the aspirin?" He glanced at the water glass she handed him.

"Oh." She walked to the bath again. "Did something happen?"

"A fire, is all."

"I had a nice evening," she said, in the bathroom.

"What doing?"

"The parlor."

"What was on?"

"Programs."

"What programs?"

"Some of the best ever."

"Who?"

"Oh, you know, the bunch."

"Yes, the bunch, the bunch, the bunch." He

pressed at the pain in his eyes and suddenly the odor
of kerosene made him vomit.

Mildred came in, humming. She was surprised.
"Why'd you do that?"

He looked with dismay at the floor. "We burnt
an old woman with her books."

"It's a good thing the rug's washable." She fetched
a mop and worked on it. "I went to Helen's last
night."

"Couldn't you get the shows in your own parlor?"

"Sure, but it's nice visiting."

She went out into the parlor. He heard her singing.

"Mildred?" he called.

She returned, singing, snapping her fingers softly.

"Aren't you going to ask me about last night?" he
said.

"What about it?"

"We burnt a thousand books. We burnt a woman."

"Well?"

The parlor was exploding with sound.

"We burnt copies of Dante and Swift and Marcus
Aurelius."

"Wasn't he a European?"

"Something like that."

"Wasn't he a radical?"

"I never read him."

"He was a radical." Mildred fiddled with the telephone. "You don't expect me to call Captain Beatty,
do you?"

"You must!"

"Don't shout!"

"I wasn't shouting." He was up in bed, suddenly,
enraged and flushed, shaking. The parlor roared in

the hot air. "I can't call him. I can't tell him I'm sick."

"Why?"

Because you're afraid, he thought. A child feigning illness, afraid to call because after a moment's discussion, the conversation would run so: "Yes, Captain, I feel better already. I'll be in at ten o'clock tonight."

"You're not sick," said Mildred.

Montag fell back in bed. He reached under his pillow. The hidden book was still there.

"Mildred, how would it be if, well, maybe I quit my job awhile?"

"You want to give up everything? After all these years of working, because, one night, some woman and her books—"

"You should have seen her, Millie!"

"She's nothing to me; she shouldn't have had books. It was her responsibility, she should've thought of that. I hate her. She's got you going and next thing you know we'll be out, no house, no job, nothing."

"You weren't there, you didn't *see*," he said. "There must be something in books, things we can't imagine, to make a woman stay in a burning house; there must be something there. You don't stay for nothing."

"She was simple-minded."

"She was as rational as you and I, more so perhaps, and we burnt her."

"That's water under the bridge."

"No, not water; fire. You ever seen a burnt house? It smolders for days. Well, this fire'll last me the rest of my life. God! I've been trying to put it out, in my mind, all night. I'm crazy with trying."

"You should've thought of that before becoming a fireman."

"Thought!" he said. "Was I given a choice? My grandfather and father were firemen. In my sleep, I ran after them."

The parlor was playing a dance tune.

"This is the day you go on the early shift," said Mildred. "You should've gone two hours ago. I just noticed."

"It's not just the woman that died," said Montag. "Last night I thought about all the kerosene I've used in the past ten years. And I thought about books. And for the first time I realized that a man was behind each one of the books. A man had to think them up. A man had to take a long time to put them down on paper. And I'd never even thought that thought before." He got out of bed.

"It took some man a lifetime maybe to put some of his thoughts down, looking around at the world and life, and then I come along in two minutes and boom! it's all over."

"Let me alone," said Mildred. "I didn't do anything."

"Let you alone! That's all very well, but how can I leave myself alone? We need not to be let alone. We need to be really bothered once in a while. How long is it since you were *really* bothered? About something important, about something real?"

And then he shut up, for he remembered last week and the two white stones staring up at the ceiling and the pump-snake with the probing eye and the two soap-faced men with the cigarettes moving in their mouths when they talked. But that was another Mildred, that was a Mildred so deep inside this one, and so bothered, really bothered, that the two women had never met. He turned away.

Mildred said, "Well, now you've done it. Out front of the house. Look who's here."

"I don't care."

"There's a phoenix car just drove up and a man in a black shirt with an orange snake stitched on his arm coming up the front walk."

"Captain Beatty?" he said.

"Captain Beatty."

Montag did not move, but stood looking into the cold whiteness of the wall immediately before him.

"Go let him in, will you? Tell him I'm sick."

"Tell him yourself!" She ran a few steps this way, a few steps that, and stopped, eyes wide, when the front door speaker called her name, softly, softly, Mrs. Montag, Mrs. Montag, someone here, someone here, Mrs. Montag, Mrs. Montag, someone's here. Fading.

Montag made sure the book was well hidden behind the pillow, climbed slowly back into bed, arranged the covers over his knees and across his chest, half sitting, and after a while Mildred moved and went out of the room and Captain Beatty strolled in, his hands in his pockets.

"Shut the 'relatives' up," said Beatty, looking around at everything except Montag and his wife.

This time, Mildred ran. The yammering voices stopped yelling in the parlor.

Captain Beatty sat down in the most comfortable chair with a peaceful look on his ruddy face. He took time to prepare and light his brass pipe and puff out a great smoke cloud. "Just thought I'd come by and see how the sick man is."

"How'd you guess?"

Beatty smiled his smile which showed the candy pinkness of his gums and the tiny candy whiteness of his teeth. "I've seen it all. You were going to call for a night off."

Montag sat in bed.

"Well," said Beatty, "*take* the night off!" He examined his eternal matchbox, the lid of which said GUARANTEED: ONE MILLION LIGHTS IN THIS IGNITER, and began to strike the chemical match abstractedly, blow out, strike, blow out, strike, speak a few words, blow out. He looked at the flame. He blew, he looked at the smoke. "When will you be well?"

"Tomorrow. The next day maybe. First of the week."

Beatty puffed his pipe. "Every fireman, sooner or later, hits this. They only need understanding, to know how the wheels run. Need to know the history of our profession. They don't feed it to rookies like they used to. Damn shame." Puff. "Only fire chiefs remember it now." Puff. "I'll let you in on it."

Mildred fidgeted.

Beatty took a full minute to settle himself in and think back for what he wanted to say.

"When did it all start, you ask, this job of ours, how did it come about, where, when? Well, I'd say it really got started around about a thing called the Civil War. Even though our rule book claims it was founded earlier. The fact is we didn't get along well until photography came into its own. Then—motion pictures in the early twentieth century. Radio. Television. Things began to have *mass*."

Montag sat in bed, not moving.

"And because they had mass, they became simpler," said Beatty. "Once, books appealed to a few people, here, there, everywhere. They could afford to be different. The world was roomy. But then the world got full of eyes and elbows and mouths. Double, triple, quadruple population. Films and radios, magazines, books leveled down to a sort of pastepudding norm, do you follow me?"

"I think so."

Beatty peered at the smoke pattern he had put out on the air. "Picture it. Nineteenth-century man with his horses, dogs, carts, slow motion. Then, in the twentieth century, speed up your camera. Books cut shorter. Condensations. Digests. Tabloids. Everything boils down to the gag, the snap ending."

"Snap ending," Mildred nodded.

"Classics cut to fit fifteen-minute radio shows, then cut again to fill a two-minute book column, winding up at last as a ten- or twelve-line dictionary resume. I exaggerate, of course. The dictionaries were for reference. But many were those whose sole knowledge of *Hamlet* (you know the title certainly, Montag; it is probably only a faint rumor of a title to you, Mrs. Montag) whose sole knowledge, as I say, of *Hamlet* was a one-page digest in a book that claimed: *now at last you can read all the classics; keep up with your neighbors.* Do you see? Out of the nursery into the college and back to the nursery; there's your intellectual pattern for the past five centuries or more."

Mildred rose and began to move around the room, picking things up and putting them down. Beatty ignored her and continued:

"Speed up the film, Montag, quick. *Click, Pic, Look, Eye, Now, Flick, Here, There, Swift, Pace, Up, Down, In, Out, Why, How, Who, What, Where, Eh? Uh! Bang! Smack! Wallop, Bing, Bong, Boom!* Digest-digests, digest-digest-digests. Politics? One column, two sentences, a headline! Then, in midair, all vanishes! Whirl man's mind around about so fast under the pumping hands of publishers, exploiters, broadcasters that the centrifuge flings off all unnecessary, time-wasting thought!"

Mildred smoothed the bedclothes. Montag felt his heart jump and jump again as she patted his pillow. Right now she was pulling at his shoulder to try to get him to move so she could take the pillow out and fix it nicely and put it back. And perhaps cry out and stare or simply reach down her hand and say, "What's this?" and hold up the hidden book with touching innocence.

"School is shortened, discipline relaxed, philosophies, histories, languages dropped, English and spelling gradually gradually neglected, finally almost completely ignored. Life is immediate, the job counts, pleasure lies all about after work. Why learn anything save pressing buttons, pulling switches, fitting nuts and bolts?"

"Let me fix your pillow," said Mildred.

"No!" whispered Montag.

"The zipper displaces the button and a man lacks just that much time to think while dressing at dawn, a philosophical hour, and thus a melancholy hour."

Mildred said, "Here."

"Get away," said Montag.

"Life becomes one big pratfall, Montag; everything bang, boff, and wow!"

59

"Wow," said Mildred, yanking at the pillow.

"For God's sake, let me be!" cried Montag passionately.

Beatty opened his eyes wide.

Mildred's hand had frozen behind the pillow. Her fingers were tracing the book's outline and as the shape became familiar her face looked surprised and then stunned. Her mouth opened to ask a question...

"Empty the theaters save for clowns and furnish the rooms with glass walls and pretty colors running up and down the walls like confetti or blood or sherry or sauterne. You like baseball, don't you, Montag?"

"Baseball's a fine game."

Now Beatty was almost invisible, a voice somewhere behind a screen of smoke.

"What's this?" asked Mildred, almost with delight. Montag heaved back against her arms. "What's this here?"

"Sit down!" Montag shouted. She jumped away, her hands empty. "We're talking!"

Beatty went on as if nothing had happened. "You like bowling, don't you, Montag?"

"Bowling, yes."

"And golf?"

"Golf is a fine game."

"Basketball?"

"A fine game."

"Billiards, pool? Football?"

"Fine games, all of them."

"More sports for everyone, group spirit, fun, and you don't have to think, eh? Organize and organize and superorganize super-super sports. More cartoons in books. More pictures. The mind drinks less and less. Impatience. Highways full of crowds going somewhere, somewhere, somewhere, nowhere. The gasoline refugee. Towns turn into motels, people in nomadic surges from place to place, following the moon tides, living tonight in the room where you slept this noon and I the night before."

Mildred went out of the room and slammed the door. The parlor "aunts" began to laugh at the parlor "uncles."

"Now let's take up the minorities in our civilization, shall we? Bigger the population, the more minorities. Don't step on the toes of the dog lovers, the cat lovers, doctors, lawyers, merchants, chiefs, Mormons, Baptists, Unitarians, second-generation Chinese, Swedes, Italians, Germans, Texans, Brooklynites, Irishmen, people from Oregon or Mexico. The people in this book, this play, this TV serial are not meant to represent any actual painters, cartographers, mechanics anywhere. The bigger your market, Montag, the less you handle controversy, remember that! All the minor minor minorities with their navels to be kept clean. Authors, full of evil thoughts, lock up your typewriters. They *did*. Magazines became a nice blend of vanilla tapioca. Books, so the damned snobbish critics said, were dishwater. No *wonder* books stopped selling, the critics said. But the public, knowing what it wanted, spinning happily, let the comic books survive. And the three-dimensional sex magazines, of course. There you have it, Montag. It didn't come from the Government down. There was no dictum, no declaration, no censorship, to start with, no! Technology, mass exploitation, and minority pressure carried the trick,

61

thank God. Today, thanks to them, you can stay happy all the time, you are allowed to read comics, the good old confessions, or trade journals."

"Yes, but what about the firemen, then?" asked Montag.

"Ah." Beatty leaned forward in the faint mist of smoke from his pipe. "What more easily explained and natural? With school turning out more runners, jumpers, racers, tinkerers, grabbers, snatchers, fliers, and swimmers instead of examiners, critics, knowers, and imaginative creators, the word 'intellectual,' of course, became the swear word it deserved to be. You always dread the unfamiliar. Surely you remember the boy in your own school class who was exceptionally 'bright,' did most of the reciting and answering while the others sat like so many leaden idols, hating him. And wasn't it this bright boy you selected for beatings and tortures after hours? Of course it was. We must all be alike. Not everyone born free and equal, as the Constitution says, but everyone *made* equal. Each man the image of every other; then all are happy, for there are no mountains to make them cower, to judge themselves against. So! A book is a loaded gun in the house next door. Burn it. Take the shot from the weapon. Breach man's mind. Who knows who might be the target of the well-read man? Me? I won't stomach them for a minute. And so when houses were finally fireproofed completely, all over the world (you were correct in your assumption the other night) there was no longer need of firemen for the old purposes. They were given the new job, as custodians of our peace of mind, the focus of our understandable and rightful dread of being inferior: official censors, judges, and executors. That's you, Montag, and that's me."

The door to the parlor opened and Mildred stood there looking in at them, looking at Beatty and then at Montag. Behind her the walls of the room were flooded with green and yellow and orange fireworks sizzling and bursting to some music composed almost completely of trap drums, tom-toms, and cymbals. Her mouth moved and she was saying something but the sound covered it.

Beatty knocked his pipe into the palm of his pink hand, studied the ashes as if they were a symbol to be diagnosed, and searched for meaning.

"You must understand that our civilization is so vast that we can't have our minorities upset and stirred. Ask yourself, What do we want in this country, above all? People want to be happy, isn't that right? Haven't you heard it all your life? I want to be happy, people say. Well, aren't they? Don't we keep them moving, don't we give them fun? That's all we live for, isn't it? For pleasure, for titillation? And you must admit our culture provides plenty of these."

"Yes."

Montag could lip-read what Mildred was saying in the doorway. He tried not to look at her mouth, because then Beatty might turn and read what was there, too.

"Colored people don't like *Little Black Sambo.* Burn it. White people don't feel good about *Uncle Tom's Cabin.* Burn it. Someone's written a book on tobacco and cancer of the lungs? The cigarette people are weeping? Burn the book. Serenity, Montag. Peace, Montag. Take your fight outside. Better yet, into the incinerator. Funerals are unhappy and pagan? Eliminate them, too. Five minutes after a person is dead he's on his way to the Big Flue, the Incinerators serviced by helicopters all over the country. Ten minutes after death a man's a speck of black dust. Let's not quibble over individuals with memoriams. Forget them. Burn all, burn everything. Fire is bright and fire is clean."

The fireworks died in the parlor behind Mildred. She had stopped talking at the same time; a miraculous coincidence. Montag held his breath.

"There was a girl next door," he said, slowly. "She's gone now, I think, dead. I can't even remember her face. But she was different. How—how did she *happen?*"

Beatty smiled. "Here or there, that's bound to occur. Clarisse McClellan? We've a record on her family. We've watched them carefully. Heredity and environment are funny things. You can't rid yourselves of all the odd ducks in just a few years. The home environment can undo a lot you try to do at school. That's why we've lowered the kindergarten age year after year until now we're almost snatching them from the cradle. We had some false alarms on the McClellans, when they lived in Chicago. Never found a book. Uncle had a mixed record; antisocial. The girl? She was a time bomb. The family had been feeding her subconscious, I'm sure, from what I saw of her school record. She didn't want to know *how* a thing was done, but *why*. That can be embarrassing. You ask why to a lot of things and you wind up very unhappy indeed, if you keep at it. The poor girl's better off dead."

"Yes, dead."

"Luckily, queer ones like her don't happen often. We know how to nip most of them in the bud, early. You can't build a house without nails and wood. If you don't want a house built, hide the nails and wood. If you don't want a man unhappy politically, don't give him two sides to a question to worry him; give him one. Better yet, give him none. Let him forget there is such a thing as war. If the government is inefficient, topheavy, and tax-mad, better it be all those than that people worry over it. Peace, Montag. Give the people contests they win by remembering the words to more popular songs or the names of state capitals or how much corn Iowa grew last year. Cram them full of noncombustible data, chock them so damned full of 'facts' they feel stuffed, but absolutely 'brilliant' with information. Then they'll feel they're thinking, they'll get a *sense* of motion without moving. And they'll be happy, because facts of that sort don't change. Don't give them any slippery stuff like philosophy or sociology to tie things up with. That way lies melancholy. Any man who can take a TV wall apart and put it back together again, and most men can, nowadays, is happier than any man who tries to slide-rule, measure, and equate the universe, which just won't be measured or equated without making man feel bestial and lonely. I know, I've tried it; to hell with it. So bring on your clubs and parties, your acrobats and magicians, your daredevils, jet cars, motorcycle helicopters, your sex and heroin, more of everything to do with automatic reflex. If the drama is bad, if the film says nothing, if the play is hollow, sting me with the theremin, loudly. I'll think I'm responding to the play, when it's only a tactile reaction to vibra-

65

tion. But I don't care. I just like solid entertainment."

Beatty got up. "I must be going. Lecture's over. I hope I've clarified things. The important thing for you to remember, Montag, is we're the Happiness Boys, the Dixie Duo, you and I and the others. We stand against the small tide of those who want to make everyone unhappy with conflicting theory and thought. We have our fingers in the dike. Hold steady. Don't let the torrent of melancholy and drear philosophy drown our world. We depend on you. I don't think you realize how important *you* are, *we* are, to our happy world as it stands now."

Beatty shook Montag's limp hand. Montag still sat, as if the house were collapsing about him and he could not move, in the bed. Mildred had vanished from the door.

"One last thing," said Beatty. "At least once in his career, every fireman gets an itch. What do the books *say,* he wonders. Oh, to *scratch* that itch, eh? Well, Montag, take my word for it, I've had to read a few in my time, to know what I was about, and the books say *nothing!* Nothing you can teach or believe. They're about nonexistent people, figments of imagination, if they're fiction. And if they're nonfiction, it's worse, one professor calling another an idiot, one philosopher screaming down another's gullet. All of them running about, putting out the stars and extinguishing the sun. You come away lost."

"Well, then, what if a fireman accidentally, really not intending anything, takes a book home with him?"

Montag twitched. The open door looked at him with its great vacant eye.

"A natural error. Curiosity alone," said Beatty.

"We don't get overanxious or mad. We let the fireman keep the book twenty-four hours. If he hasn't burned it by then, we simply come burn it for him."

"Of course." Montag's mouth was dry.

"Well, Montag. Will you take another, later shift, today? Will we see you tonight perhaps?"

"I don't know," said Montag.

"What?" Beatty looked faintly surprised.

Montag shut his eyes. "I'll be in later. Maybe."

"We'd certainly miss you if you didn't show," said Beatty, putting his pipe in his pocket thoughtfully.

I'll never come in again, thought Montag.

"Get well and keep well," said Beatty.

He turned and went out through the open door.

Montag watched through the window as Beatty drove away in his gleaming yellow-flame-colored beetle with the black, char-colored tires.

Across the street and down the way the other houses stood with their flat fronts. What was it Clarisse had said one afternoon? "No front porches. My uncle says there used to be front porches. And people sat there sometimes at night, talking when they wanted to talk, rocking, and not talking when they didn't want to talk. Sometimes they just sat there and thought about things, turned things over. My uncle says the architects got rid of the front porches because they didn't look well. But my uncle says that was merely rationalizing it; the real reason, hidden underneath, might be they didn't want people sitting like that, doing nothing, rocking, talking; that was the wrong *kind* of social life. People talked too much. And they had time to think. So they ran off with the porches. And the gardens, too. Not many gardens any more to sit around in. And look at the furniture. No rocking chairs any more. They're too comfortable. Get people up and running around. My uncle says . . . and . . . my uncle . . . and . . . my uncle . . ." Her voice faded.

Montag turned and looked at his wife, who sat in the middle of the parlor talking to an announcer, who in turn was talking to her. "Mrs. Montag," he was saying. This, that, and the other. "Mrs. Montag—" Something else and still another. The converter attachment, which had cost them one hundred dollars, automatically supplied her name whenever the announcer addressed his anonymous audience, leaving a blank where the proper syllables could be filled in. A special spot-wavex-scrambler also caused his televised image, in the area immediately about his lips, to mouth the vowels and consonants beautifully. He was a friend, no doubt of it, a good friend. "Mrs. Montag—now look right here."

Her head turned. Though she quite obviously was not listening.

Montag said, "It's only a step from not going to work today to not working tomorrow, to not working at the firehouse ever again."

"You are going to work tonight, though, aren't you?" said Mildred.

"I haven't decided. Right now I've got an awful feeling I want to smash things and kill things."

"Go take the beetle."

"No, thanks."

"The keys to the beetle are on the night table. I always like to drive fast when I feel that way. You get it up around ninety-five and you feel wonderful.

Sometimes I drive all night and come back and you don't know it. It's fun out in the country. You hit rabbits, sometimes you hit dogs. Go take the beetle."

"No, I don't want to, this time. I want to hold onto this funny thing. God, it's gotten big on me. I don't know what it is. I'm so damned unhappy, I'm so mad, and I don't know why. I feel like I'm putting on weight. I feel fat. I feel like I've been saving up a lot of things, and don't know what. I might even start reading books."

"They'd put you in jail, wouldn't they?" She looked at him as if he were behind the glass wall.

He began to put on his clothes, moving restlessly about the bedroom. "Yes, and it might be a good idea. Before I hurt someone. Did you hear Beatty? Did you listen to him? He knows all the answers. He's right. Happiness is important. Fun is everything. And yet I kept sitting there saying to myself, I'm not happy, I'm not happy."

"*I* am." Mildred's mouth beamed. "And proud of it."

"I'm going to do something," said Montag. "I don't even know what yet, but I'm going to do something big."

"I'm tired of listening to this junk," said Mildred, turning from him to the announcer again.

Montag touched the volume control in the wall and the announcer was speechless.

"Millie?" He paused. "This is your house as well as mine. I feel it's only fair that I tell you something now. I should have told you before, but I wasn't even admitting it to myself. I have something I want you to see, something I've put away and hid during the past year, now and again, once in a while, I didn't know why, but I did it and I never told you."

He took hold of a straight-backed chair and moved it slowly and steadily into the hall near the front door and climbed up on it and stood for a moment like a statue on a pedestal, his wife standing under him, waiting. Then he reached up and pulled back the grille of the air-conditioning system and reached far back inside to the right and moved still another sliding sheet of metal and took out a book. Without looking at it he dropped it to the floor. He put his hand back up and took out two books and moved his hand down and dropped the two books to the floor. He kept moving his hand and dropping books, small ones, fairly large ones, yellow, red, green ones. When he was done he looked down upon some twenty books lying at his wife's feet.

"I'm sorry," he said. "I didn't really think. But now it looks as if we're in this together."

Mildred backed away as if she were suddenly confronted by a pack of mice that had come up out of the floor. He could hear her breathing rapidly and her face was paled out and her eyes were fastened wide. She said his name over, twice, three times. Then, moaning, she ran forward, seized a book, and ran toward the kitchen incinerator.

He caught her, shrieking. He held her and she tried to fight away from him, scratching.

"No, Millie, no! Wait! Stop it, will you? You don't know . . . stop it!" He slapped her face, he grabbed her again and shook her.

She said his name and began to cry.

"Millie!" he said. "Listen. Give me a second, will you? We can't do anything. We can't burn these. I want to look at them, at least look at them once.

Then if what the Captain says is true, we'll burn them together, believe me, we'll burn them together. You must help me." He looked down into her face and took hold of her chin and held her firmly. He was looking not only at her, but for himself and what he must do, in her face. "Whether we like this or not, we're in it. I've never asked for much from you in all these years, but I ask it now, I plead for it. We've got to start somewhere here, figuring out why we're in such a mess, you and the medicine nights, and the car, and me and my work. We're heading right for the cliff, Millie. God, I don't want to go over. This isn't going to be easy. We haven't anything to go on, but maybe we can piece it out and figure it and help each other. I need you so much right now, I can't tell you. If you love me at all you'll put up with this, twenty-four, forty-eight hours, that's all I ask, then it'll be over, I promise, I swear! And if there is something here, just one little thing out of a whole mess of things, maybe we can pass it on to someone else."

She wasn't fighting any more, so he let her go. She sagged away from him and slid down the wall and sat on the floor looking at the books. Her foot touched one and she saw this and pulled her foot away.

"That woman, the other night, Millie, you weren't there. You didn't see her face. And Clarisse. You never talked to her. I talked to her. And men like Beatty are afraid of her. I can't understand it. Why should they be so afraid of someone like her? But I kept putting her alongside the firemen in the House last night, and I suddenly realized I didn't like them at all, and I didn't like myself at all any more. And

I thought maybe it would be best if the firemen themselves were burnt."

"Guy!"

The front door voice called softly:

"Mrs. Montag, Mrs. Montag, someone here, someone here, Mrs. Montag, Mrs. Montag, someone here."

Softly.

They turned to stare at the door and the books toppled everywhere, everywhere in heaps.

"Beatty!" said Mildred.

"It can't be him."

"He's come back!" she whispered.

The front door voice called again softly. "Someone here . . ."

"We won't answer." Montag lay back against the wall and then slowly sank to a crouching position and began to nudge the books, bewilderedly, with his thumb, his forefinger. He was shivering and he wanted above all to shove the books up through the ventilator again, but he knew he could not face Beatty again. He crouched and then he sat and the voice of the front door spoke again, more insistently. Montag picked a single small volume from the floor. "Where do we begin?" He opened the book halfway and peered at it. "We begin by beginning, I guess."

"He'll come in," said Mildred, "and burn us and the books!"

The front door voice faded at last. There was a silence. Montag felt the presence of someone beyond the door, waiting, listening. Then the footsteps going away down the walk and over the lawn.

"Let's see what this is," said Montag.

He spoke the words haltingly and with a terrible

self-consciousness. He read a dozen pages here or there and came at last to this:

" 'It is computed that eleven thousand persons have at several times suffered death rather than submit to break their eggs at the smaller end.' "

Mildred sat across the hall from him. "What does it mean? It doesn't mean *anything!* The Captain was right!"

"Here now," said Montag. "We'll start over again, at the beginning."

PART TWO

The Sieve and
the Sand

They read the long afternoon through, while the cold November rain fell from the sky upon the quiet house. They sat in the hall because the parlor was so empty and gray-looking without its wall lit with orange and yellow confetti and skyrockets and women in gold-mesh dresses and men in black velvet pulling one-hundred-pound rabbits from silver hats. The parlor was dead and Mildred kept peering in at it with a blank expression as Montag paced the floor and came back and squatted down and read a page as many as ten times, aloud.

" 'We cannot tell the precise moment when friendship is formed. As in filling a vessel drop by drop, there is at last a drop which makes it run over; so in a series of kindnesses there is at last one which makes the heart run over.' "

Montag sat listening to the rain.

"Is that what it was in the girl next door? I've tried so hard to figure."

"She's dead. Let's talk about someone alive, for goodness' sake."

Montag did not look back at his wife as he went trembling along the hall to the kitchen, where he stood a long time watching the rain hit the windows before he came back down the hall in the gray light, waiting for the tremble to subside.

He opened another book.

" 'That favourite subject, Myself.' "

He squinted at the wall. " 'That favourite subject, Myself.' "

"I understand *that* one," said Mildred.

"But Clarisse's favorite subject wasn't herself. It was everyone else, and me. She was the first person in a good many years I've really liked. She was the first person I can remember who looked straight at me as if I counted." He lifted the two books. "These men have been dead a long time, but I know their words point, one way or another, to Clarisse."

Outside the front door, in the rain, a faint scratching.

Montag froze. He saw Mildred thrust herself back to the wall and gasp.

"Someone—the door—why doesn't the door-voice tell us—"

"I shut it off."

Under the doorsill, a slow, probing sniff, an exhalation of electric steam.

Mildred laughed. "It's only a dog, that's what! You want me to shoo him away?"

"Stay where you are!"

Silence. The cold rain falling. And the smell of blue electricity blowing under the locked door.

"Let's get back to work," said Montag, quietly.

Mildred kicked at a book. "Books aren't people. You read and I look all around, but there isn't *anybody!*"

He stared at the parlor that was dead and gray as the waters of an ocean that might teem with life if they switched on the electronic sun.

"Now," said Mildred, "my 'family' is people. They tell me things; *I* laugh, *they* laugh! And the colors!"

"Yes, I know."

"And besides, if Captain Beatty knew about those books—" She thought about it. Her face grew amazed and then horrified. "He might come and burn the house and the 'family.' That's awful! Think of our investment. Why should I read? What *for?*"

"What for! Why!" said Montag. "I saw the damnedest snake in the world the other night. It was dead but it was alive. It could see but it couldn't see. You want to *see* that snake? It's at Emergency Hospital where they filed a report on all the junk the snake got out of you! Would you like to go and check their file? Maybe you'd look under Guy Montag or maybe under Fear or War. Would you like to go to that house that burnt last night? And rake ashes for the bones of the woman who set fire to her own house! What about Clarisse McClellan, where do we look for her? The morgue! Listen!"

The bombers crossed the sky and crossed the sky over the house, gasping, murmuring, whistling like an immense, invisible fan, circling in emptiness.

"Jesus God," said Montag. "Every hour so many

damn things in the sky! How in hell did those bombers get up there every single second of our lives! Why doesn't someone want to talk about it! We've started and won two atomic wars since 1990! Is it because we're having so much fun at home we've forgotten the world? Is it because we're so rich and the rest of the world's so poor and we just don't care if they are? I've heard rumors; the world is starving, but we're well fed. Is it true, the world works hard and we play? Is that why we're hated so much? I've heard the rumors about hate, too, once in a long while, over the years. Do *you* know why? *I* don't, that's *sure!* Maybe the books can get us half out of the cave. They just *might* stop us from making the same damn insane mistakes! I don't hear those idiot bastards in your parlor talking about it. God, Millie, don't you *see?* An hour a day, two hours, with these books, and maybe . . ."

The telephone rang. Mildred snatched the phone.

"Ann!" She laughed. "Yes, the White Clown's on tonight!"

Montag walked to the kitchen and threw the book down. "Montag," he said, "you're really stupid. Where do we go from here? Do we turn the books in, forget it?" He opened the book to read over Mildred's laughter.

Poor Millie, he thought. Poor Montag, it's mud to you, too. But where do you get help, where do you find a teacher this late?

Hold on. He shut his eyes. Yes, of course. Again he found himself thinking of the green park a year ago. The thought had been with him many times recently but now he remembered how it was that day in the city park when he had seen that old man in the black suit hide something, quickly, in his coat. . . . The old man leapt up as if to run. And Montag said, "Wait!"

"I haven't done anything!" cried the old man, trembling.

"No one said you did."

They had sat in the green soft light without saying a word for a moment and then Montag talked about the weather and then the old man responded with a pale voice. It was a strange quiet meeting. The old man admitted to being a retired English Professor who had been thrown out upon the world forty years ago when the last liberal arts college shut for lack of students and patronage. His name was Faber, and when he finally lost his fear of Montag, he talked in a cadenced voice, looking at the sky and the trees and the green park, and when an hour had passed he said something to Montag and Montag sensed it was a rhymeless poem. Then the old man grew even more courageous and said something else and that was a poem, too. Faber held his hand over his left coat pocket and spoke these words gently, and Montag knew if he reached out, he might pull a book of poetry from the man's coat. But he did not reach out. His hands stayed on his knees, numbed and useless. "I don't talk *things,* sir," said Faber. "I talk the *meaning* of things. I sit here and *know* I'm alive."

That was all there was to it, really. An hour of monologue, a poem, a comment, and then without either acknowledging the fact that Montag was a fireman, Faber, with a certain trembling, wrote his address on a slip of paper. "For your file," he said, "in case you decide to be angry with me."

"I'm not angry," Montag said, surprised.

Mildred shrieked with laughter in the hall.

Montag went to his bedroom closet and flipped through his file-wallet to the heading: FUTURE IN-VESTIGATIONS (?). Faber's name was there. He hadn't turned it in and he hadn't erased it.

He dialed the call on a secondary phone. The phone on the far end of the line called Faber's name a dozen times before the professor answered in a faint voice. Montag identified himself and was met with a lengthy silence. "Yes, Mr. Montag?"

"Professor Faber, I have a rather odd question to ask. How many copies of the Bible are left in this country?"

"I don't know what you're talking about!"

"I want to know if there are *any* copies left at all."

"This is some sort of trap! I can't talk to just *any-one* on the phone!"

"How many copies of Shakespeare and Plato?"

"None! You know as well as I do. None!"

Faber hung up.

Montag put down the phone. None. A thing he knew of course from the firehouse listings. But some-how he had wanted to hear it from Faber himself.

In the hall Mildred's face was suffused with ex-citement. "Well, the ladies are coming over!"

Montag showed her a book. "This is the Old and New Testament, and . . ."

"Don't start that again!"

"It might be the last copy in this part of the world."

"You've got to hand it back tonight, don't you? Captain Beatty *knows* you got it, doesn't he?"

"I don't think he knows *which* book I stole. But how do I choose a substitute? Do I turn in Mr. Jefferson? Mr. Thoreau? Which is least valuable? If I pick a substitute and Beatty does know which book I stole, he'll guess we've an entire library here!"

Mildred's mouth twitched. "See what you're *doing*? You'll ruin us! Who's more important, me or that Bible?" She was beginning to shriek now, sitting there like a wax doll melting in its own heat.

He could hear Beatty's voice. "Sit down, Montag. Watch. Delicately, like the petals of a flower. Light the first page, light the second page. Each becomes a black butterfly. Beautiful, eh? Light the third page from the second and so on, chain smoking, chapter by chapter, all the silly things the words mean, all the false promises, all the second-hand notions and time-worn philosophies." There sat Beatty, perspiring gently, the floor littered with swarms of black moths that had died in a single storm.

Mildred stopped screaming as quickly as she started. Montag was not listening. "There's only one thing to do," he said. "Sometime before tonight when I give the book to Beatty, I've got to have a duplicate made."

"You'll be here for the White Clown tonight, and the ladies coming over?" cried Mildred.

Montag stopped at the door, with his back turned. "Millie?"

A silence. "What?"

"Millie? Does the White Clown love you?"

No answer.

"Millie, does—" He licked his lips. "Does your

'family' love you, love you *very* much, love you with all their heart and soul, Millie?"

He felt her blinking slowly at the back of his neck. "Why'd you ask a silly question like that?"

He felt he wanted to cry, but nothing would happen to his eyes or his mouth.

"If you see that dog outside," said Mildred, "give him a kick for me."

He hesitated, listening at the door. He opened it and stepped out.

The rain had stopped and the sun was setting in the clear sky. The street and the lawn and the porch were empty. He let his breath go in a great sigh.

He slammed the door.

He was on the subway.

I'm numb, he thought. When did the numbness really begin in my face? In my body? The night I kicked the pill bottle in the dark, like kicking a buried mine.

The numbness will go away, he thought. It'll take time, but I'll do it, or Faber will do it for me. Someone somewhere will give me back the old face and the old hands the way they were. Even the smile, he thought, the old burnt-in smile, that's gone. I'm lost without it.

The subway fled past him, cream tile, jet-black, cream tile, jet-black, numerals and darkness, more darkness and the total adding itself.

Once as a child he had sat upon a yellow dune by the sea in the middle of the blue and hot summer day, trying to fill a sieve with sand, because some cruel cousin had said, "Fill this sieve and you'll get a dime!" And the faster he poured, the faster it sifted through with a hot whispering. His hands were tired, the sand was boiling, the sieve was empty. Seated there in the midst of July, without a sound, he felt the tears move down his cheeks.

Now as the vacuum-underground rushed him through the dead cellars of town, jolting him, he remembered the terrible logic of that sieve, and he looked down and saw that he was carrying the Bible open. There were people in the suction train but he held the book in his hands and the silly thought came to him, if you read fast and read all, maybe some of the sand will stay in the sieve. But he read and the words fell through, and he thought, in a few hours, there will be Beatty, and here will be me handing this over, so no phrase must escape me, each line must be memorized. I will myself to do it.

He clenched the book in his fists.

Trumpets blared.

"Denham's Dentifrice."

Shut up, thought Montag. Consider the lilies of the field.

"Denham's Dentifrice."

They toil not—

"Denham's—"

Consider the lilies of the field, shut up, shut up.

"Dentifrice!"

He tore the book open and flicked the pages and felt of them as if he were blind, he picked at the shape of the individual letters, not blinking.

"Denham's. Spelled: D-E-N—"

They toil not, neither do they . . .

A fierce whisper of hot sand through empty sieve.

"Denham's does it!"

Consider the lilies, the lilies, the lilies . . .

"Denham's dental detergent."

"Shut up, shut up, shut up!" It was a plea, a cry so terrible that Montag found himself on his feet, the shocked inhabitants of the loud car staring, moving back from this man with the insane, gorged face, the gibbering, dry mouth, the flapping book in his fist. The people who had been sitting a moment before, tapping their feet to the rhythm of Denham's Dentifrice, Denham's Dandy Dental Detergent, Denham's Dentifrice Dentifrice Dentifrice, one two, one two three, one two, one two three. The people whose mouths had been faintly twitching the words Dentifrice Dentifrice Dentifrice. The train radio vomited upon Montag, in retaliation, a great tonload of music made of tin, copper, silver, chromium, and brass. The people were pounded into submission; they did not run, there was no place to run; the great air train fell down its shaft in the earth.

"Lilies of the field."

"Denham's."

"*Lilies,* I said!"

The people stared.

"Call the guard."

"The man's off—"

"Knoll View!"

The train hissed to its stop.

"Knoll View!" A cry.

"Denham's." A whisper.

Montag's mouth barely moved. "Lilies . . ."

The train door whistled open. Montag stood. The door gasped, started shut. Only then did he leap past the other passengers, screaming in his mind, plunge through the slicing door only in time. He ran on the white tiles up through the tunnels, ignoring the escalators, because he wanted to feel his feet move, arms swing, lungs clench, unclench, feel his throat go raw with air. A voice drifted after him, "Denham's Denham's Denham's," the train hissed like a snake. The train vanished in its hole.

"Who is it?"
"Montag out here."
"What do you want?"
"Let me in."
"I haven't done anything!"
"I'm alone, dammit!"
"You swear it?"
"I swear!"

The front door opened slowly. Faber peered out, looking very old in the light and very fragile and very much afraid. The old man looked as if he had not been out of the house in years. He and the white plaster walls inside were much the same. There was white in the flesh of his mouth and his cheeks and his hair was white and his eyes had faded, with white in the vague blueness there. Then his eyes touched on the book under Montag's arm and he did not look so old any more and not quite as fragile. Slowly, his fear went.

"I'm sorry. One has to be careful."

He looked at the book under Montag's arm and could not stop. "So it's true."

Montag stepped inside. The door shut.

"Sit down." Faber backed up, as if he feared the book might vanish if he took his eyes from it. Behind him, the door to a bedroom stood open, and in that room a litter of machinery and steel tools were strewn upon a desktop. Montag had only a glimpse, before Faber, seeing Montag's attention diverted, turned quickly and shut the bedroom door and stood holding the knob with a trembling hand. His gaze returned unsteadily to Montag, who was now seated with the book in his lap. "The book—where did you—?"

"I stole it."

Faber, for the first time, raised his eyes and looked directly into Montag's face. "You're brave."

"No," said Montag. "My wife's dying. A friend of mine's already dead. Someone who may have been a friend was burnt less than twenty-four hours ago. You're the only one I knew might help me. To see. To see . . ."

Faber's hands itched on his knees. "May I?"

"Sorry." Montag gave him the book.

"It's been a long time. I'm not a religious man. But it's been a long time." Faber turned the pages, stopping here and there to read. "It's as good as I remember. Lord, how they've changed it in our 'parlors' these days. Christ is one of the 'family' now. I often wonder if God recognizes His own son the way we've dressed him up, or is it dressed him down? He's a regular peppermint stick now, all sugar-crystal and saccharine when he isn't making veiled references to certain commercial products that every worshiper *absolutely* needs." Faber sniffed the book. "Do you know that books smell like nutmeg or some spice from a foreign land? I loved to smell them when I was a boy. Lord, there were a lot of lovely books once, before we let them go." Faber turned the pages. "Mr. Montag, you are looking at a coward. I saw the way things were going, a long time back. I said nothing. I'm one of the innocents who could have spoken up and out when no one would listen to the 'guilty,' but I did not speak and thus became guilty myself. And when finally they set the structure to burn the books, using the firemen, I grunted a few times and subsided, for there were no others grunting or yelling with me, by then. Now it's too late." Faber closed the Bible. "Well—suppose you tell me why you came here?"

"Nobody listens any more. I can't talk to the walls because they're yelling at *me*. I can't talk to my wife; she listens to the *walls*. I just want someone to hear what I have to say. And maybe if I talk long enough, it'll make sense. And I want you to teach me to understand what I read."

Faber examined Montag's thin, blue-jowled face. "How did you get shaken up? What knocked the torch out of your hands?"

"I don't know. We have everything we need to be happy, but we aren't happy. Something's missing. I looked around. The only thing I positively *knew* was gone was the books I'd burned in ten or twelve years. So I thought books might help."

"You're a hopeless romantic," said Faber. "It would be funny if it were not serious. It's not books you need, it's some of the things that once were in books. The same things *could* be in the 'parlor families' today. The same infinite detail and awareness could be projected through the radios and televisors, but are not. No, no, it's not books at all you're looking for! Take it where you can find it, in old phonograph records, old motion pictures, and in old friends; look for it in nature and look for it in yourself. Books were only one type of receptacle where we stored a lot of things we were afraid we might forget. There is nothing magical in them at all. The magic is only in what books say, how they stitched the patches of the universe together into one garment for us. Of course you couldn't know this, of course you still can't understand what I mean when I say all this. You are intuitively right, that's what counts. Three things are missing.

"Number one: Do you know why books such as this are so important? Because they have quality. And what does the word quality mean? To me it means texture. This book has *pores*. It has features. This book can go under the microscope. You'd find life under the glass, streaming past in infinite profusion. The more pores, the more truthfully recorded details of life per square inch you can get on a sheet of paper, the more 'literary' you are. That's *my* definition, anyway. *Telling detail. Fresh* detail. The good writers touch life often. The mediocre ones run a quick hand over her. The bad ones rape her and leave her for the flies.

"So now do you see why books are hated and feared? They show the pores in the face of life. The comfortable people want only wax moon faces, poreless, hairless, expressionless. We are living in a time when flowers are trying to live on flowers, instead of growing on good rain and black loam. Even fireworks, for all their prettiness, come from the chemistry of the earth. Yet somehow we think we can grow, feeding on flowers and fireworks, without completing the cycle back to reality. Do you know the legend of Hercules and Antaeus, the giant wrestler, whose strength was incredible so long as he stood firmly on the earth? But when he was held, rootless, in midair, by Hercules, he perished easily. If there isn't something in that legend for us today, in this city, in our time, then I am completely insane. Well, there we have the first thing I said we needed. Quality, texture of information."

"And the second?"

"Leisure."

"Oh, but we've plenty of off-hours."

"Off-hours, yes. But time to think? If you're not driving a hundred miles an hour, at a clip where you can't think of anything else but the danger, then you're playing some game or sitting in some room where you can't argue with the four-wall televisor. Why? The televisor is 'real.' It is immediate, it has dimension. It tells you what to think and blasts it in. It *must* be right. It *seems* so right. It rushes you on so quickly to its own conclusions your mind hasn't time to protest, 'What nonsense!' "

"Only the 'family' is 'people.' "

"I beg pardon?"

"My wife says books aren't 'real.' "

"Thank God for that. You can shut them, say, 'Hold on a moment.' You play God to it. But who has ever torn himself from the claw that encloses you when you drop a seed in a TV parlor? It grows you any shape it wishes! It is an environment as real as the world. It *becomes* and *is* the truth. Books can be beaten down with reason. But with all my knowledge and skepticism, I have never been able to argue with a one-hundred-piece symphony orchestra, full color, three dimensions, and being in and part of those incredible parlors. As you see, my parlor is nothing but four plaster walls. And here." He held out two small rubber plugs. "For my ears when I ride the subway jets."

"Denham's Dentifrice; they toil not, neither do they spin," said Montag, eyes shut. "Where do we go from here? Would books help us?"

"Only if the third necessary thing could be given us. Number one, as I said: quality of information. Number two: leisure to digest it. And number three: the right to carry out actions based on what we learn from the interaction of the first two. And I hardly think a very old man and a fireman turned sour could *do* much this late in the game . . ."

"I can *get* books."

"You're running a risk."

"That's the good part of dying; when you've nothing to lose, you run any risk you want."

"There, you've said an interesting thing," laughed Faber, "without having read it!"

"Are things like *that* in books? But it came off the top of my mind!"

"All the better. You didn't fancy it up for me or anyone, even yourself."

Montag leaned forward. "This afternoon I thought that if it turned out that books *were* worthwhile, we might get a press and print some extra copies—"

"We?"

"You and I."

"Oh, no!" Faber sat up.

"But let me tell you my plan—"

"If you insist on telling me, I must ask you to leave."

"But aren't *you* interested?"

"Not if you start talking the sort of talk that might get me burnt for my trouble. The only way I could *possibly* listen to you would be if somehow the fireman structure itself could be burnt. Now, if you suggest that we print extra books and arrange to have them hidden in firemen's houses all over the country, so that seeds of suspicion would be sown among these arsonists, bravo, I'd say!"

"Plant the books, turn in an alarm, and see the firemen's houses burn, is that what you mean?"

Faber raised his brows and looked at Montag as if he were seeing a new man. "I was joking."

"If you thought it would be a plan worth trying, I'd have to take your word it would help."

"You can't guarantee things like that! After all, when we *had* all the books we needed, we still insisted on finding the highest cliff to jump off. But we *do* need a breather. We *do* need knowledge. And perhaps in a thousand years we might pick smaller cliffs to jump off. The books are to remind us what asses and fools we are. They're Caesar's praetorian guard, whispering as the parade roars down the avenue, 'Remember, Caesar, thou art mortal.' Most of us can't rush around, talk to everyone, know all the cities of the world, we haven't time, money or that many friends. The things you're looking for, Montag, are in the world, but the only way the average chap will ever see ninety-nine per cent of them is in a book. Don't ask for guarantees. And don't look to be saved in any *one* thing, person, machine, or library. Do your own bit of saving, and if you drown, at least die knowing you were headed for shore."

Faber got up and began to pace the room.

"Well?" asked Montag.

"You're absolutely serious?"

"Absolutely."

"It's an insidious plan, if I do say so myself."

Faber glanced nervously at his bedroom door. "To see the firehouses burn across the land, destroyed as hotbeds of treason. The salamander devours his tail! Ho, God!"

"I've a list of firemen's residences everywhere. With some sort of underground—"

"Can't trust people, that's the dirty part. You and I and who else will set the fires?"

"Aren't there professors like yourself, former writers, historians, linguists? . . ."

"Dead or ancient."

"The older the better; they'll go unnoticed. You know dozens, admit it!"

"Oh, there are many actors alone who haven't acted Pirandello or Shaw or Shakespeare for years because their plays are too *aware* of the world. We could use their anger. And we could use the honest rage of those historians who haven't written a line for forty years. True, we might form classes in thinking and reading."

"Yes!"

"But that would just nibble the edges. The whole culture's shot through. The skeleton needs melting and reshaping. Good God, it isn't as simple as just picking up a book you laid down half a century ago. Remember, the firemen are rarely necessary. The public itself stopped reading of its own accord. You firemen provide a circus now and then at which buildings are set off and crowds gather for the pretty blaze, but it's a small sideshow indeed, and hardly necessary to keep things in line. So few want to be rebels any more. And out of those few, most, like myself, scare easily. Can you dance faster than the White Clown, shout louder than 'Mr. Gimmick' and the parlor 'families'? If you can, you'll win your way, Montag. In any event, you're a fool. People are having *fun*."

"Committing suicide! Murdering!"

A bomber flight had been moving east all the time they talked, and only now did the two men stop and listen, feeling the great jet sound tremble inside themselves.

"Patience, Montag. Let the war turn off the 'families.' Our civilization is flinging itself to pieces. Stand back from the centrifuge."

"There has to be someone ready when it blows up."

"What? Men quoting Milton? Saying, I remember Sophocles? Reminding the survivors that man has his good side, too? They will only gather up their stones to hurl at each other. Montag, go home. Go to bed. Why waste your final hours racing about your cage denying you're a squirrel?"

"Then you don't care any more?"

"I care so much I'm sick."

"And you won't help me?"

"Good night, good night."

Montag's hands picked up the Bible. He saw what his hands had done and he looked surprised.

"Would you like to own this?"

Faber said, "I'd give my right arm."

Montag stood there and waited for the next thing to happen. His hands, by themselves, like two men working together, began to rip the pages from the book. The hands tore the fly-leaf and then the first and then the second page.

"Idiot, what're you doing!" Faber sprang up, as if he had been struck. He fell against Montag. Montag

warded him off and let his hands continue. Six more
pages fell to the floor. He picked them up and
wadded the paper under Faber's gaze.

"Don't, oh, don't!" said the old man.

"Who can stop me? I'm a fireman. I can burn
you!"

The old man stood looking at him. "You
wouldn't."

"I could!"

"The book. Don't tear it any more." Faber sank
into a chair, his face very white, his mouth trembling.
"Don't make me feel any more tired. What do you
want?"

"I need you to teach me."

"All right, all right."

Montag put the book down. He began to unwad
the crumpled paper and flatten it out as the old man
watched tiredly.

Faber shook his head as if he were waking up.

"Montag, have you any money?"

"Some. Four, five hundred dollars. Why?"

"Bring it. I know a man who printed our college
paper half a century ago. That was the year I came
to class at the start of the new semester and found
only one student to sign up for Drama from Aeschy-
lus to O'Neill. You see? How like a beautiful statue
of ice it was, melting in the sun. I remember the
newspapers dying like huge moths. No one *wanted*
them back. No one missed them. And then the Government, seeing how advantageous it was to have
people reading only about passionate lips and the
fist in the stomach, circled the situation with your
fire-eaters. So, Montag, there's this unemployed
printer. We might start a few books, and wait on the

war to break the pattern and give us the push we need. A few bombs and the 'families' in the walls of all the houses, like harlequin rats, will shut up! In the silence, our stage whisper might carry."

They both stood looking at the book on the table.

"I've tried to remember," said Montag. "But, hell, it's gone when I turn my head. God, how I want something to say to the Captain. He's read enough so he has all the answers, or seems to have. His voice is like butter. I'm afraid he'll talk me back the way I was. Only a week ago, pumping a kerosene hose, I thought: God, what fun!"

The old man nodded. "Those who don't build must burn. It's as old as history and juvenile delinquents."

"So that's what I am."

"There's some of it in all of us."

Montag moved toward the front door. "Can you help me in any way tonight, with the Fire Captain? I need an umbrella to keep off the rain. I'm so damned afraid I'll drown if he gets me again."

The old man said nothing, but glanced once more, nervously, at his bedroom. Montag caught the glance. "Well?"

The old man took a deep breath, held it, and let it out. He took another, eyes closed, his mouth tight, and at last exhaled. "Montag . . ."

The old man turned at last and said, "Come along. I would actually have let you walk right out of my house. I *am* a cowardly old fool."

Faber opened the bedroom door and let Montag into a small chamber where stood a table upon which a number of metal tools lay among a welter of microscopic wire-hairs, tiny coils, bobbins, and crystals.

"What's this?" asked Montag.

"Proof of my terrible cowardice. I've lived alone so many years, throwing images on walls with my imagination. Fiddling with electronics, radio transmission, has been my hobby. My cowardice is of such a passion, complementing the revolutionary spirit that lives in its shadow, I was forced to design *this*."

He picked up a small green metal object no larger than a .22 bullet.

"I paid for all this—how? Playing the stock market, of course, the last refuge in the world for the dangerous intellectual out of a job. Well, I played the market and built all this and I've waited. I've waited, trembling, half a lifetime for someone to speak to me. I dared speak to no one. That day in the park when we sat together, I knew that someday you might drop by, with fire or friendship, it was hard to guess. I've had this little item ready for months. But I almost let you go, I'm *that* afraid!"

"It looks like a Seashell Radio."

"And something more! It *listens!* If you put it in your ear, Montag, I can sit comfortably home, warming my frightened bones, and hear and analyze the firemen's world, find its weaknesses, without danger. I'm the Queen Bee, safe in the hive. You will be the drone, the traveling ear. Eventually, I could put out ears into all parts of the city, with various men, listening and evaluating. If the drones die, I'm still safe at home, tending my fright with a maximum of comfort and a minimum of chance. See how safe I play it, how contemptible I am?"

Montag placed the green bullet in his ear. The old man inserted a similar object in his own ear and moved his lips.

"Montag!"

The voice was in Montag's head.

"I *hear* you!"

The old man laughed. "You're coming over fine, too!" Faber whispered, but the voice in Montag's head was clear. "Go to the firehouse when it's time. I'll be with you. Let's listen to this Captain Beatty together. He could be one of us. God knows. I'll give you things to say. We'll give him a good show. Do you hate me for this electronic cowardice of mine? Here I am sending you out into the night, while I stay behind the lines with my damned ears listening for you to get your head chopped off."

"We all do what we do," said Montag. He put the Bible in the old man's hands. "Here. I'll chance turning in a substitute. Tomorrow——"

"I'll see the unemployed printer, yes; *that* much I can do."

"Good night, Professor."

"Not good night. I'll be with you the rest of the night, a vinegar gnat tickling your ear when you need me. But good night and good luck, anyway."

The door opened and shut. Montag was in the dark street again, looking at the world.

You could feel the war getting ready in the sky that night. The way the clouds moved aside and came back, and the way the stars looked, a million of them swimming between the clouds, like the enemy discs, and the feeling that the sky might fall upon the city and turn it to chalk dust, and the moon go up in red fire; that was how the night felt.

Montag walked from the subway with the money in his pocket (he had visited the bank, which was open all night every night with robot tellers in attendance) and as he walked he was listening to the Seashell Radio in one ear . . . "We have mobilized a million men. Quick victory is ours if the war comes . . ." Music flooded over the voice quickly and it was gone.

"Ten million men mobilized," Faber's voice whispered in his other ear. "But *say* one million. It's happier."

"Faber?"

"Yes?"

"I'm not thinking. I'm just doing like I'm told, like always. You said get the money and I got it. I didn't really think of it myself. When do I start working things out on my own?"

"You've started already, by saying what you just said. You'll have to take me on faith."

"I took the others on faith!"

"Yes, and look where we're headed. You'll have to travel blind for a while. Here's my arm to hold onto."

"I don't want to change sides and just be *told* what to do. There's no reason to change if I do that."

"You're wise already!"

Montag felt his feet moving him on the sidewalk toward his house. "Keep talking."

"Would you like me to read? I'll read so you can remember. I go to bed only five hours a night. Nothing to do. So if you like, I'll read you to sleep nights. They say you retain knowledge even when you're sleeping, if someone whispers it in your ear."

"Yes."

"Here." Far away across town in the night, the faintest whisper of a turned page. "The Book of Job."

The moon rose in the sky as Montag walked, his lips moving just a trifle.

He was eating a light supper at nine in the evening when the front door cried out in the hall and Mildred ran from the parlor like a native fleeing an eruption of Vesuvius. Mrs. Phelps and Mrs. Bowles came through the front door and vanished into the volcano's mouth with martinis in their hands. Montag stopped eating. They were like a monstrous crystal chandelier tinkling in a thousand chimes, he saw their Cheshire Cat smiles burning through the walls of the house, and now they were screaming at each other above the din.

Montag found himself at the parlor door with his food still in his mouth.

"Doesn't everyone look nice!"

"Nice."

"You look fine, Millie!"

"Fine."

"Everyone looks swell."

"Swell!"

Montag stood watching them.

"Patience," whispered Faber.

"I shouldn't be here," whispered Montag, almost to himself. "I should be on my way back to you with the money!"

"Tomorrow's time enough. Careful!"

"Isn't this show *wonderful?*" cried Mildred.

"Wonderful!"

On one wall a woman smiled and drank orange

juice simultaneously. How does she do both at once? thought Montag, insanely. In the other walls an x-ray of the same woman revealed the contracting journey of the refreshing beverage on its way to her delighted stomach! Abruptly the room took off on a rocket flight into the clouds, it plunged into a lime-green sea where blue fish ate red and yellow fish. A minute later, Three White Cartoon Clowns chopped off each other's limbs to the accompaniment of immense incoming tides of laughter. Two minutes more and the room whipped out of town to the jet cars wildly circling an arena, bashing and backing up and bashing each other again. Montag saw a number of bodies fly in the air.

"Millie, did you *see* that!"

"I saw it, I *saw* it!"

Montag reached inside the parlor wall and pulled the main switch. The images drained away, as if the water had been let from a gigantic crystal bowl of hysterical fish.

The three women turned slowly and looked with unconcealed irritation and then dislike at Montag.

"When do you suppose the war will start?" he said. "I notice your husbands aren't here tonight?"

"Oh they come and go, come and go," said Mrs. Phelps. "In again out again Finnegan, the Army called Pete yesterday. He'll be back next week. The Army said so. Quick war. Forty-eight hours, they said, and everyone home. That's what the Army said. Quick war. Pete was called yesterday and they said he'd be back next week. Quick . . ."

The three women fidgeted and looked nervously at the empty mud-colored walls.

"I'm not worried," said Mrs. Phelps. "I'll let

Pete do all the worrying." She giggled. "I'll let old Pete do all the worrying. Not me. I'm not worried."

"Yes," said Millie. "Let old Pete do the worrying."

"It's always someone else's husband dies, they say."

"I've heard that, too. I've never known any dead man killed in a war. Killed jumping off buildings, yes, like Gloria's husband last week, but from wars? No."

"Not from wars," said Mrs. Phelps. "Anyway, Pete and I always said, no tears, nothing like that. It's our third marriage each and we're independent. Be independent, we always said. He said, if I get killed off, you just go right ahead and don't cry, but get married again, and don't think of me."

"That reminds me," said Mildred. "Did you see that Clara Dove five-minute romance last night in your wall? Well, it was all about this woman who—"

Montag said nothing but stood looking at the women's faces as he had once looked at the faces of saints in a strange church he had entered when he was a child. The faces of those enameled creatures meant nothing to him, though he talked to them and stood in that church for a long time, trying to be of that religion, trying to know what that religion was, trying to get enough of the raw incense and special dust of the place into his lungs and thus into his blood to feel touched and concerned by the meaning of the colorful men and women with the porcelain eyes and the blood-ruby lips. But there was nothing, nothing; it was a stroll through another store, and his currency strange and unusable there, and his passion cold, even when he touched the wood and plaster and clay. So it was now, in his own parlor, with these women twisting in their chairs under his gaze, lighting cigarettes, blowing smoke, touching their sun-fired hair and examining their blazing fingernails as if they had caught fire from his look. Their faces grew haunted with silence. They leaned forward at the sound of Montag's swallowing his final bite of food. They listened to his feverish breathing. The three empty walls of the room were like the pale brows of sleeping giants now, empty of dreams. Montag felt that if you touched these three staring brows you would feel a fine salt sweat on your fingertips. The perspiration gathered with the silence and the subaudible trembling around and about and in the women who were burning with tension. Any moment they might hiss a long sputtering hiss and explode.

Montag moved his lips.

"Let's talk."

The women jerked and stared.

"How're your children, Mrs. Phelps?" he asked.

"You know I haven't any! No one in his right mind, the good Lord knows, would have children!" said Mrs. Phelps, not quite sure why she was angry with this man.

"I wouldn't say that," said Mrs. Bowles. "I've had *two* children by Caesarian section. No use going through all that agony for a baby. The world must reproduce, you know, the race must go on. Besides, they sometimes look just like you, and that's nice. Two Caesarians turned the trick, yes, sir. Oh, my doctor said, Caesarians aren't necessary; you've got the hips for it, everything's normal, but I *insisted.*"

"Caesarians or not, children are ruinous; you're out of your mind," said Mrs. Phelps.

"I plunk the children in school nine days out of ten. I put up with them when they come home three days a month; it's not bad at all. You heave them into the 'parlor' and turn the switch. It's like washing clothes: stuff laundry in and slam the lid." Mrs. Bowles tittered. "They'd just as soon kick as kiss me. Thank God, I can kick back!"

The women showed their tongues, laughing.

Mildred sat a moment and then, seeing that Montag was still in the doorway, clapped her hands. "Let's talk politics, to please Guy!"

"Sounds fine," said Mrs. Bowles. "I voted last election, same as everyone, and I laid it on the line for President Noble. I think he's one of the nicest-looking men ever became president."

"Oh, but the man they ran against him!"

"He wasn't much, was he? Kind of small and homely and he didn't shave too close or comb his hair very well."

"What possessed the 'Outs' to run him? You just don't go running a little short man like that against a tall man. Besides—he mumbled. Half the time I couldn't hear a word he said. And the words I *did* hear I didn't understand!"

"Fat, too, and didn't dress to hide it. No wonder the landslide was for Winston Noble. Even their names helped. Compare Winston Noble to Hubert Hoag for ten seconds and you can almost figure the results."

"Damn it!" cried Montag. "What do you know about Hoag and Noble!"

"Why, they were right in that parlor wall, not six

months ago. One was always picking his nose; it drove me wild."

"Well, Mr. Montag," said Mrs. Phelps, "do you want us to vote for a man like that?"

Mildred beamed. "You just run away from the door, Guy, and don't make us nervous."

But Montag was gone and back in a moment with a book in his hand.

"Guy!"

"Damn it all, damn it all, damn it!"

"What've you got there; isn't that a book? I thought that all special training these days was done by film." Mrs. Phelps blinked. "You reading up on fireman theory?"

"Theory, hell," said Montag. "It's poetry."

"Montag." A whisper.

"Leave me alone!" Montag felt himself turning in a great circling roar and buzz and hum.

"Montag, hold on, don't . . ."

"Did you *hear* them, did you hear these monsters talking about monsters? Oh God, the way they jabber about people and their own children and themselves and the way they talk about their husbands and the way they talk about war, dammit, I stand here and I can't believe it!"

"I didn't say a single word about any *war*, I'll have you know," said Mrs. Phelps.

"As for poetry, I hate it," said Mrs. Bowles.

"Have you ever heard any?"

"Montag," Faber's voice scraped away at him. "You'll ruin everything. Shut up, you fool!"

All three women were on their feet.

"Sit down!"

They sat.

"I'm going home," quavered Mrs. Bowles.

"Montag, Montag, please, in the name of God, what're you up to?" pleaded Faber.

"Why don't you just read us one of those poems from your little book." Mrs. Phelps nodded. "I think that'd be very interesting."

"That's not right," wailed Mrs. Bowles. "We can't do that!"

"Well, look at Mr. Montag, he wants to, I know he does. And if we listen nice, Mr. Montag will be happy and then maybe we can go on and do something else." She glanced nervously at the long emptiness of the walls enclosing them.

"Montag, go through with this and I'll cut off, I'll leave." The beetle jabbed his ear. "What good is this, what'll you prove!"

"Scare hell out of them, that's what, scare the living daylights out!"

Mildred looked at the empty air. "Now, Guy, just *who* are you talking to?"

A silver needle pierced his brain. "Montag, listen, only one way out, play it as a joke, cover up, pretend you aren't mad at all. Then—walk to your wall incinerator, and throw the book in!"

Mildred had already anticipated this in a quavery voice. "Ladies, once a year, every fireman's allowed to bring one book home, from the old days, to show his family how silly it all was, how nervous that sort of thing can make you, how crazy. Guy's surprise tonight is to read you one sample to show how mixed-up things were, so none of us will ever have to bother our little old heads about that junk again, isn't that *right*, darling?"

He crushed the book in his fists.

"Say 'yes.' "

His mouth moved like Faber's:

"Yes."

Mildred snatched the book with a laugh. "Here! Read this one. No, I take it back. Here's that real funny one you read out loud today. Ladies, you won't understand a word. It goes umpty-tumpty-ump. Go ahead, Guy, that page, dear."

He looked at the opened page.

A fly stirred its wings softly in his ear. "Read."

"What's the title, dear?"

"*Dover Beach*." His mouth was numb.

"Now read in a nice clear voice and go *slow*."

The room was blazing hot, he was all fire, he was all coldness; they sat in the middle of an empty desert with three chairs and him standing, swaying, and him waiting for Mrs. Phelps to stop straightening her dress hem and Mrs. Bowles to take her fingers away from her hair. Then he began to read in a low, stumbling voice that grew firmer as he progressed from line to line, and his voice went out across the desert, into the whiteness, and around the three sitting women there in the great hot emptiness.

" 'The Sea of Faith
    Was once, too, at the full, and round earth's
       shore
    Lay like the folds of a bright girdle furled.
    But now I only hear
    Its melancholy, long, withdrawing roar,
    Retreating, to the breath
    Of the night-wind, down the vast edges drear
    And naked shingles of the world.' "

The chairs creaked under the three women.
Montag finished it out:

" 'Ah, love, let us be true
   To one another! for the world, which seems
   To lie before us like a land of dreams,
   So various, so beautiful, so new,
   Hath really neither joy, nor love, nor light,
   Nor certitude, nor peace, nor help for pain;
   And we are here as on a darkling plain
   Swept with confused alarms of struggle and
      flight,
   Where ignorant armies clash by night.' "

Mrs. Phelps was crying.

The others in the middle of the desert watched her crying grow very loud as her face squeezed itself out of shape. They sat, not touching her, bewildered with her display. She sobbed uncontrollably. Montag himself was stunned and shaken.

"Sh, sh," said Mildred. "You're all right, Clara, now, Clara, snap out of it! Clara, what's *wrong?*"

"I—I," sobbed Mrs. Phelps, "don't know, don't know, I just don't know, oh, oh . . ."

Mrs. Bowles stood up and glared at Montag. "You see? I knew it, that's what I wanted to prove! I knew it would happen! I've always said, poetry and tears, poetry and suicide and crying and awful feelings, poetry and sickness; *all* that mush! Now I've had it proved to me. You're nasty, Mr. Montag, you're *nasty!*"

Faber said, "Now . . ."

Montag felt himself turn and walk to the wall slot

and drop the book in through the brass notch to the waiting flames.

"Silly words, silly words, silly awful hurting words," said Mrs. Bowles. "Why *do* people want to hurt people? Not enough hurt in the world, you got to tease people with stuff like that!"

"Clara, now, Clara," begged Mildred, pulling her arm. "Come on, let's be cheery, you turn the 'family' on now. Go ahead. Let's laugh and be happy now, stop crying, we'll have a party!"

"No," said Mrs. Bowles. "I'm trotting right straight home. You want to visit my house and my 'family,' well and good. But I won't come in this fireman's crazy house again in my lifetime!"

"Go home." Montag fixed his eyes upon her, quietly. "Go home and think of your first husband divorced and your second husband killed in a jet and your third husband blowing his brains out, go home and think of the dozen abortions you've had, go home and think of that and your damn Caesarian sections, too, and your children who hate your guts! Go home and think how it all happened and what did you ever do to stop it? Go home, go home!" he yelled. "Before I knock you down and kick you out the door!"

Doors slammed and the house was empty. Montag stood alone in the winter weather, with the parlor walls the color of dirty snow.

In the bathroom, water ran. He heard Mildred shake the sleeping tablets into her hand.

"Fool, Montag, fool, fool, oh God you silly fool..."

"Shut up!" He pulled the green bullet from his ear and jammed it into his pocket.

It sizzled faintly. ". . . fool . . . fool . . ."

He searched the house and found the books where Mildred had stacked them behind the refrigerator. Some were missing and he knew that she had started on her own slow process of dispersing the dynamite in her house, stick by stick. But he was not angry now, only exhausted and bewildered with himself. He carried the books into the backyard and hid them in the bushes near the alley fence. For tonight only, he thought, in case she decides to do any more burning.

He went back through the house. "Mildred?" He called at the door of the darkened bedroom. There was no sound.

Outside, crossing the lawn, on his way to work, he tried not to see how completely dark and deserted Clarisse McClellan's house was . . .

On the way downtown he was so completely alone with his terrible error that he felt the necessity for the strange warmness and goodness that came from a familiar and gentle voice speaking in the night. Already, in a few short hours, it seemed that he had known Faber a lifetime. Now he knew that he was two people, that he was, above all, Montag who knew nothing, who did not even know himself a fool, but only suspected it. And he knew that he was also the old man who talked to him and talked to him as the train was sucked from one end of the night city to the other on one long sickening gasp of motion. In the days to follow, and in the nights when there was no moon and in the nights when there was a very bright moon shining on the earth, the old man would go on with this talking and this talking, drop by drop, stone by stone, flake by flake.

His mind would well over at last and he would not be Montag any more, this the old man told him, assured him, promised him. He would be Montag-plus-Faber, fire plus water, and then, one day, after everything had mixed and simmered and worked away in silence, there would be neither fire nor water, but wine. Out of two separate and opposite things, a third. And one day he would look back upon the fool and know the fool. Even now he could feel the start of the long journey, the leave-taking, the going-away from the self he had been.

It was good listening to the beetle hum, the sleepy mosquito buzz and delicate filigree murmur of the old man's voice at first scolding him and then consoling him in the late hour of night as he emerged from the steaming subway toward the firehouse world.

"Pity, Montag, pity. Don't haggle and nag them; you were so recently *of* them yourself. They are so confident that they will run on forever. But they won't run on. They don't know that this is all one huge big blazing meteor that makes a pretty fire in space, but that someday it'll have to *hit*. They see only the blaze, the pretty fire, as you saw it.

"Montag, old men who stay at home, afraid, tending their peanut-brittle bones, have no right to criticize. Yet you almost killed things at the start. Watch it! I'm with you, remember that. I understand how it happened. I must admit that your blind raging invigorated me. God, how young I felt! But now—I want you to feel old, I want a little of my cowardice to be distilled in you tonight. The next few hours, when you see Captain Beatty, tiptoe 'round him, let *me* hear him for you, let *me* feel the situation out.

Survival is our ticket. Forget the poor, silly women . . ."

"I made them unhappier than they have been in years, I think," said Montag. "It shocked me to see Mrs. Phelps cry. Maybe they're right, maybe it's best not to face things, to run have fun. I don't know. I feel guilty—"

"No, you mustn't! If there were no war, if there was peace in the world, I'd say fine, *have* fun! But, Montag, you mustn't go back to being just a fireman. All *isn't* well with the world."

Montag perspired.

"Montag, you listening?"

"My feet," said Montag. "I can't move them. I feel so damn silly. My feet won't move!"

"Listen. Easy now," said the old man gently. "I know, I know. You're afraid of making mistakes. *Don't* be. Mistakes can be profited by. Man, when I was younger I *shoved* my ignorance in people's faces. They beat me with sticks. By the time I was forty my blunt instrument had been honed to a fine cutting point for me. If you hide your ignorance, no one will hit you and you'll never learn. Now, pick up your feet, into the firehouse with you! We're twins, we're not alone any more, we're not separated out in different parlors, with no contact between. If you need help when Beatty pries at you, I'll be sitting right here in your eardrum making notes!"

Montag felt his right foot, then his left foot, move.

"Old man," he said, "stay *with* me."

The Mechanical Hound was gone. Its kennel was empty and the firehouse stood all about in plaster silence and the orange Salamander slept with its kerosene in its belly and the fire throwers crossed upon its flanks and Montag came in through the silence and touched the brass pole and slid up in the dark air, looking back at the deserted kennel, his heart beating, pausing, beating. Faber was a gray moth asleep in his ear, for the moment.

Beatty stood near the drophole waiting, but with his back turned as if he were not waiting.

"Well," he said to the men playing cards, "here comes a very strange beast which in all tongues is called a fool."

He put his hand to one side, palm up, for a gift. Montag put the book in it. Without even glancing at the title, Beatty tossed the book in the trash basket and lit a cigarette. " 'Who are a little wise, the best fools be.' Welcome back, Montag. I hope you'll be staying with us, now that your fever is done and your sickness over. Sit in for a hand of poker?"

They sat and the cards were dealt. In Beatty's sight, Montag felt the guilt of his hands. His fingers were like ferrets that had done some evil and now never rested, always stirred and picked and hid in pockets, moving from under Beatty's alcohol-flame stare. If Beatty so much as breathed on them, Montag felt that his hands might wither, turn over on their sides, and never be shocked to life again; they would be buried the rest of his life in his coat sleeves, forgotten. For these were the hands that had acted on their own, no part of him, here was where the conscience first manifested itself to snatch books, dart off with Job and Ruth and Willie Shakespeare, and now, in the firehouse, these hands seemed gloved with blood.

Twice in half an hour, Montag had to rise from the

game and go to the latrine to wash his hands. When he came back he hid his hands under the table.

Beatty laughed. "Let's have your hands in sight, Montag. Not that we don't trust you, understand, but—"

They all laughed.

"Well," said Beatty, "the crisis is past and all is well, the sheep returns to the fold. We're all sheep who have strayed at times. Truth is truth, to the end of reckoning, we've cried. They are never alone that are accompanied with noble thoughts, we've shouted to ourselves. 'Sweet food of sweetly uttered knowledge,' Sir Philip Sidney said. But on the other hand: 'Words are like leaves and where they most abound, Much fruit of sense beneath is rarely found.' Alexander Pope. What do you think of that, Montag?"

"I don't know."

"Careful," whispered Faber, living in another world, far away.

"Or this? 'A little learning is a dangerous thing. Drink deep, or taste not the Pierian spring; There shallow draughts intoxicate the brain, and drinking largely sobers us again.' Pope. Same Essay. Where does that put you?"

Montag bit his lip.

"I'll tell you," said Beatty, smiling at his cards. "That made you for a little while a drunkard. Read a few lines and off you go over the cliff. Bang, you're ready to blow up the world, chop off heads, knock down women and children, destroy authority. I know, I've been through it all."

"I'm all right," said Montag, nervously.

"Stop blushing. I'm not needling, really I'm not. Do you know, I had a dream an hour ago. I lay down for a catnap and in this dream you and I, Montag, got into a furious debate on books. You towered with rage, yelled quotes at me. I calmly parried every thrust. *Power,* I said. And you, quoting Dr. Johnson, said, 'Knowledge is more than equivalent to force!' And I said, 'Well, Dr. Johnson also said, dear boy, that "He is no wise man that will quit a certainty for an uncertainty."' Stick with the firemen, Montag. All else is dreary chaos!"

"Don't listen," whispered Faber. "He's trying to confuse. He's slippery. Watch out!"

Beatty chuckled. "And you said, quoting, 'Truth will come to light, murder will not be hid long!' And I cried in good humor, 'Oh God, he speaks only of his horse!' And 'The Devil can cite Scripture for his purpose.' And you yelled, 'This age thinks better of a gilded fool than of a threadbare saint in wisdom's school!' And I whispered gently, 'The dignity of truth is lost with much protesting.' And you screamed, 'Carcasses bleed at the sight of the murderer!' And I said, patting your hand, 'What, do I give you trench mouth?' And you shrieked, 'Knowledge is power!' and 'A dwarf on a giant's shoulders sees the farthest of the two!' and I summed my side up with rare serenity in, 'The folly of mistaking a metaphor for a proof, a torrent of verbiage for a spring of capital truths, and oneself as an oracle, is inborn in us, Mr. Valery once said.'"

Montag's head whirled sickeningly. He felt beaten unmercifully on brow, eyes, nose, lips, chin, on shoulders, on upflailing arms. He wanted to yell, "No! Shut up, you're confusing things, stop it!" Beatty's graceful fingers thrust out to seize his wrist.

"God, what a pulse! I've got you going, have I,

Montag? Jesus God, your pulse sounds like the day after the war. Everything but sirens and bells! Shall I talk some more? I like your look of panic. Swahili, Indian, English Lit., I speak them all. A kind of excellent dumb discourse, Willie!"

"Montag, hold on!" The moth brushed Montag's ear. "He's muddying the waters!"

"Oh, you were scared silly," said Beatty, "for I was doing a terrible thing in using the very books you clung to, to rebut you on every hand, on every point! What traitors books can be! You think they're backing you up, and they turn on you. Others can use them, too, and there you are, lost in the middle of the moor, in a great welter of nouns and verbs and adjectives. And at the very end of my dream, along I came with the Salamander and said, 'Going my way?' And you got in and we drove back to the firehouse in beatific silence, all dwindled away to peace." Beatty let Montag's wrist go, let the hand slump limply on the table. "All's well that is well in the end."

Silence. Montag sat like a carved white stone. The echo of the final hammer on his skull died slowly away into the black cavern where Faber waited for the echoes to subside. And then when the startled dust had settled down about Montag's mind, Faber began, softly, "All right, he's had his say. You must take it in. I'll say my say, too, in the next few hours. And you'll take it in. And you'll try to judge them and make your decision as to which way to jump, or fall. But I want it to be your decision, not mine, and not the Captain's. But remember that the Captain belongs to the most dangerous enemy to truth and freedom, the solid unmoving cattle of the majority. Oh God, the terrible tyranny of the majority. We all have our harps to play. And it's up to you now to know with which ear you'll listen."

Montag opened his mouth to answer Faber and was saved this error in the presence of others when the station bell rang. The alarm-voice in the ceiling chanted. There was a tacking-tacking sound as the alarm-report telephone typed out the address across the room. Captain Beatty, his poker cards in one pink hand, walked with exaggerated slowness to the phone and ripped out the address when the report was finished. He glanced perfunctorily at it and shoved it in his pocket. He came back and sat down. The others looked at him.

"It can wait exactly forty seconds while I take all the money away from you," said Beatty, happily.

Montag put his cards down.

"Tired, Montag? Going out of this game?"

"Yes."

"Hold on. Well, come to think of it, we can finish this hand later. Just leave your cards face down and hustle the equipment. On the double now." And Beatty rose up again. "Montag, you don't look well. I'd hate to think you were coming down with another fever . . ."

"I'll be all right."

"You'll be fine. This is a special case. Come on, jump for it!"

They leapt into the air and clutched the brass pole as if it were the last vantage point above a tidal wave passing below, and then the brass pole, to their dismay, slid them down into darkness, into the blast and cough and suction of the gaseous dragon roaring to life!

"Hey!"

They rounded a corner in thunder and siren, with concussion of tires, with scream of rubber, with a shift of kerosene bulk in the glittery brass tank, like the food in the stomach of a giant, with Montag's fingers jolting off the silver rail, swinging into cold space, with the wind tearing his hair back from his head, with the wind whistling in his teeth, and him all the while thinking of the women, the chaff women in his parlor tonight, with the kernels blown out from under them by a neon wind, and his silly damned reading of a book to them. How like trying to put out fires with waterpistols, how senseless and insane. One rage turned in for another. One anger displacing another. When would he stop being entirely mad and be quiet, be very quiet indeed?

"Here we go!"

Montag looked up. Beatty never drove, but he was driving tonight, slamming the Salamander around corners, leaning forward high on the driver's throne, his massive black slicker flapping out behind so that he seemed a great black bat flying above the engine, over the brass numbers, taking the full wind.

"Here we go to keep the world happy, Montag!"

Beatty's pink, phosphorescent cheeks glimmered in the high darkness, and he was smiling furiously.

"Here we are!"

The Salamander boomed to a halt, throwing men off in slips and clumsy hops. Montag stood fixing his raw eyes to the cold bright rail under his clenched fingers.

I can't do it, he thought. How can I go at this new assignment, how can I go on burning things? I can't go in this place.

Beatty, smelling of the wind through which he had rushed, was at Montag's elbow. "All right, Montag."

The men ran like cripples in their clumsy boots, as quietly as spiders.

At last Montag raised his eyes and turned.

Beatty was watching his face.

"Something the matter, Montag?"

"Why," said Montag slowly, "we've stopped in front of *my* house."

PART THREE

Burning Bright

ights flicked on and house doors opened all down the street, to watch the carnival set up. Montag and Beatty stared, one with dry satisfaction, the other with disbelief, at the house before them, this main ring in which torches would be juggled and fire eaten.

"Well," said Beatty, "now you *did* it. Old Montag wanted to fly near the sun and now that he's burnt his damn wings, he wonders why. Didn't I hint enough when I sent the Hound around your place?"

Montag's face was entirely numb and featureless; he felt his head turn like a stone carving to the dark place next door, set in its bright border of flowers.

Beatty snorted. "Oh, no! You weren't fooled by that little idiot's routine, now, were you? Flowers, butterflies, leaves, sunsets, oh, hell! It's all in her file. I'll be damned. I've hit the bull's-eye. Look at

123

the sick look on your face. A few grass blades and the quarters of the moon. What trash. What good did she ever *do* with all that?"

Montag sat on the cold fender of the Dragon, moving his head half an inch to the left, half an inch to the right, left, right, left, right, left . . .

"She saw everything. She didn't do anything to anyone. She just let them alone."

"Alone, hell! She chewed around you, didn't she? One of those damn do-gooders with their shocked, holier-than-thou silences, their one talent making others feel guilty. God damn, they rise like the midnight sun to sweat you in your bed!"

The front door opened; Mildred came down the steps, running, one suitcase held with a dreamlike clenching rigidity in her fist, as a beetle-taxi hissed to the curb.

"Mildred!"

She ran past with her body stiff, her face floured with powder, her mouth gone, without lipstick.

"Mildred, you *didn't* put in the alarm!"

She shoved the valise in the waiting beetle, climbed in, and sat mumbling, "Poor family, poor family, oh everything gone, everything, everything gone now . . ."

Beatty grabbed Montag's shoulder as the beetle blasted away and hit seventy miles an hour, far down the street, gone.

There was a crash like the falling parts of a dream fashioned out of warped glass, mirrors, and crystal prisms. Montag drifted about as if still another incomprehensible storm had turned him, to see Stoneman and Black wielding axes, shattering windowpanes to provide cross-ventilation.

The brush of a death's-head moth against a cold black screen. "Montag, this is Faber. Do you hear me? What's happening?"

"This is happening to *me*," said Montag.

"What a dreadful surprise," said Beatty. "For everyone nowadays knows, absolutely is *certain,* that nothing will ever happen to *me*. Others die, *I* go on. There are no consequences and no responsibilities. Except that there *are*. But let's not talk about them, eh? By the time the consequences catch up with you, it's too late, isn't it, Montag?"

"Montag, can you get away, run?" asked Faber.

Montag walked but did not feel his feet touch the cement and then the night grasses. Beatty flicked his igniter nearby and the small orange flame drew his fascinated gaze.

"What is there about fire that's so lovely? No matter what age we are, what draws us to it?" Beatty blew out the flame and lit it again. "It's perpetual motion; the thing man wanted to invent but never did. Or almost perpetual motion. If you let it go on, it'd burn our lifetimes out. What is fire? It's a mystery. Scientists give us gobbledegook about friction and molecules. But they don't really know. Its real beauty is that it destroys responsibility and consequences. A problem gets too burdensome, then into the furnace with it. Now, Montag, you're a burden. And fire will lift you off my shoulders, clean, quick, sure; nothing to rot later. Antibiotic, aesthetic, practical."

Montag stood looking in now at this queer house, made strange by the hour of the night, by murmuring neighbor voices, by littered glass, and there on the floor, their covers torn off and spilled out like swan feathers, the incredible books that looked so silly and really not worth bothering with, for these were nothing but black type and yellowed paper and raveled binding.

Mildred, of course. She must have watched him hide the books in the garden and brought them back in. Mildred. Mildred.

"I want you to do this job all by your lonesome, Montag. Not with kerosene and a match, but piece-work, with a flame thrower. Your house, your clean-up."

"Montag, can't you run, get away!"

"No!" cried Montag, helplessly. "The Hound! Because of the Hound!"

Faber heard and Beatty, thinking it was meant for him, heard. "Yes, the Hound's somewhere about the neighborhood, so don't try anything. Ready?"

"Ready." Montag snapped the safety catch on the flame thrower.

"Fire!"

A great nuzzling gout of fire leapt out to lap at the books and knock them against the wall. He stepped into the bedroom and fired twice and the twin beds went up in a great simmering whisper, with more heat and passion and light than he would have supposed them to contain. He burnt the bedroom walls and the cosmetics chest because he wanted to change every-thing, the chairs, the tables, and in the dining room the silverware and plastic dishes, everything that showed that he had lived here in this empty house with a strange woman who would forget him tomor-row, who had gone and quite forgotten him already, listening to her Seashell Radio pour in on her and in on her as she rode across town, alone. And as before, it was good to burn, he felt himself gush out in the fire, snatch, rend, rip in half with flame, and put away the senseless problem. If there was no solution, well then now there was no problem, either. Fire was best for everything!

"The books, Montag!"

The books leapt and danced like roasted birds, their wings ablaze with red and yellow feathers.

And then he came to the parlor where the great idiot monsters lay asleep with their white thoughts and their snowy dreams. And he shot a bolt at each of the three blank walls and the vacuum hissed out at him. The emptiness made an even emptier whistle, a senseless scream. He tried to think about the vacuum upon which the nothingnesses had performed, but he could not. He held his breath so the vacuum could not get into his lungs. He cut off its terrible emptiness, drew back, and gave the entire room a gift of one huge bright yellow flower of burning. The fireproof plastic sheath on everything was cut wide and the house began to shudder with flame.

"When you're quite finished," said Beatty behind him, "you're under arrest."

The house fell in red coals and black ash. It bedded itself down in sleepy pink-gray cinders and a smoke plume blew over it, rising and waving slowly back and forth in the sky. It was three-thirty in the morning. The crowd drew back into the houses; the great tents of the circus had slumped into charcoal and rubble and the show was well over.

Montag stood with the flame thrower in his limp hands, great islands of perspiration drenching his armpits, his face smeared with soot. The other firemen waited behind him, in the darkness, their faces illumined faintly by the smouldering foundation.

Montag started to speak twice and then finally managed to put his thought together.

"Was it my wife turned in the alarm?"

Beatty nodded. "But her friends turned in an alarm earlier that I let ride. One way or the other, you'd have got it. It was pretty silly, quoting poetry around free and easy like that. It was the act of a silly damn snob. Give a man a few lines of verse and he thinks he's the Lord of all Creation. You think you can walk on water with your books. Well, the world can get by just fine without them. Look where they got you, in slime up to your lip. If I stir the slime with my little finger, you'll drown!"

Montag could not move. A great earthquake had come with fire and leveled the house and Mildred was under there somewhere and his entire life under there and he could not move. The earthquake was still shaking and falling and shivering inside him and he stood there, his knees half bent under the great load of tiredness and bewilderment and outrage, letting Beatty hit him without raising a hand.

"Montag, you idiot, Montag, you damn fool; why did you *really* do it?"

Montag did not hear, he was far away, he was running with his mind, he was gone, leaving this dead soot-covered body to sway in front of another raving fool.

"Montag, get out of there!" said Faber.

Montag listened.

Beatty struck him a blow on the head that sent him reeling back. The green bullet in which Faber's voice whispered and cried fell to the sidewalk.

Beatty snatched it up, grinning. He held it half in, half out of his ear.

Montag heard the distant voice calling, "Montag, you all right?"

Beatty switched the green bullet off and thrust it in his pocket. "Well—so there's more here than I thought. I saw you tilt your head, listening. First I thought you had a Seashell. But when you turned clever later, I wondered. We'll trace this and drop it on your friend."

"No!" said Montag.

He twitched the safety catch on the flame thrower. Beatty glanced instantly at Montag's fingers and his eyes widened the faintest bit. Montag saw the surprise there and himself glanced to his hands to see what new thing they had done. Thinking back later he could never decide whether the hands or Beatty's reaction to the hands gave him the final push toward murder. The last rolling thunder of the avalanche stoned down about his ears, not touching him.

Beatty grinned his most charming grin. "Well, that's one way to get an audience. Hold a gun on a man and force him to listen to your speech. Speech away. What'll it be this time? Why don't you belch Shakespeare at me, you fumbling snob? 'There is no terror, Cassius, in your threats, for I am arm'd so strong in honesty that they pass by me as an idle wind, which I respect not!' How's that? Go ahead now, you second-hand litterateur, pull the trigger." He took one step toward Montag.

Montag only said, "We never burned *right* . . ."

"Hand it over, Guy," said Beatty with a fixed smile.

And then he was a shrieking blaze, a jumping,

129

sprawling gibbering mannikin, no longer human or known, all writhing flame on the lawn as Montag shot one continuous pulse of liquid fire on him. There was a hiss like a great mouthful of spittle banging a red-hot stove, a bubbling and frothing as if salt had been poured over a monstrous black snail to cause a terrible liquefaction and a boiling over of yellow foam. Montag shut his eyes, shouted, shouted, and fought to get his hands at his ears to clamp and to cut away the sound. Beatty flopped over and over and over, and at last twisted in on himself like a charred wax doll and lay silent.

The other two firemen did not move.

Montag kept his sickness down long enough to aim the flame thrower. "Turn around!"

They turned, their faces like blanched meat, streaming sweat; he beat their heads, knocking off their helmets and bringing them down on themselves. They fell and lay without moving.

The blowing of a single autumn leaf.

He turned and the Mechanical Hound was there.

It was half across the lawn, coming from the shadows, moving with such drifting ease that it was like a single solid cloud of black-gray smoke blown at him in silence.

It made a single last leap into the air coming down at Montag from a good three feet over his head, its spidered legs reaching, the procaine needle snapping out its single angry tooth. Montag caught it with a bloom of fire, a single wondrous blossom that curled in petals of yellow and blue and orange about the metal dog, clad it in a new covering as it slammed into Montag and threw him ten feet back against the bole of a tree, taking the flame gun with him. He felt it scrabble and seize his leg and stab the needle in for a moment before the fire snapped the Hound up in the air, burst its metal bones at the joints, and blew out its interior in a single flushing of red color like a skyrocket fastened to the street. Montag lay watching the dead-alive thing fiddle the air and die. Even now it seemed to want to get back at him and finish the injection which was now working through the flesh of his leg. He felt all of the mingled relief and horror at having pulled back only in time to have just his knee slammed by the fender of a car hurtling by at ninety miles an hour. He was afraid to get up, afraid he might not be able to gain his feet at all, with an anesthetized leg. A numbness in a numbness hollowed into a numbness . . .

And now? . . .

The street empty, the house burnt like an ancient bit of stage scenery, the other homes dark, the Hound here, Beatty there, the two other firemen another place, and the Salamander? . . . He gazed at the immense engine. That would have to go, too.

Well, he thought, let's see how badly off you are. On your feet now. Easy, easy . . . *there*.

He stood and he had only one leg. The other was like a chunk of burnt pine log he was carrying along as a penance for some obscure sin. When he put his weight on it, a shower of silver needles gushed up the length of the calf and went off in the knee. He wept. Come on! Come on, you, you can't stay here!

A few house lights were going on again down the street, whether from the incidents just passed or because of the abnormal silence following the fight, Montag did not know. He hobbled around the ruins, seizing at his bad leg when it lagged, talking and whimpering and shouting directions at it and cursing it and pleading with it to work for him now when it was vital. He heard a number of people crying out in the darkness and shouting. He reached the back-yard and the alley. Beatty, he thought, you're not a problem now. You always said, don't face a prob-lem, burn it. Well, now I've done both. Good-bye, Captain.

And he stumbled along the alley in the dark.

A shotgun blast went off in his leg every time he put it down and he thought, you're a fool, a damn fool, an awful fool, an idiot, an awful idiot, a damn idiot, and a fool, a damn fool; look at the mess and where's the mop, look at the mess and what do you do? Pride, dammit, and temper, and you've junked it all, at the very start you vomit on everyone and on yourself. But everything at once, but everything one on top of another, Beatty, the women, Mildred, Clarisse, everything. No excuse, though, no excuse. A fool, a damn fool, go give yourself up!

No, we'll save what we can, we'll do what there is left to do. If we have to burn, let's take a few more with us. Here!

He remembered the books and turned back. Just on the off chance.

He found a few books where he had left them, near the garden fence. Mildred, God bless her, had missed a few. Four books still lay hidden where he had put them. Voices were wailing in the night and flashbeams swirled about. Other Salamanders were roaring, their engines far away, and police sirens were cutting their way across town with their sirens.

Montag took the four remaining books and hopped, jolted, hopped his way down the alley and suddenly fell as if his head had been cut off and only his body lay there. Something inside had jerked him to a halt and flopped him down. He lay where he had fallen and sobbed, his legs folded, his face pressed blindly to the gravel.

Beatty wanted to die.

In the middle of the crying Montag knew it for the truth. Beatty had wanted to die. He had just stood there, not really trying to save himself, just stood there, joking, needling, thought Montag, and the thought was enough to stifle his sobbing and let him pause for air. How strange, strange, to want to die so much that you let a man walk around armed and then instead of shutting up and staying alive, you go on yelling at people and making fun of them until you get them mad, and then . . .

At a distance, running feet.

Montag sat up. Let's get out of here. Come on, get up, get up, you just can't sit! But he was still crying and that had to be finished. It was going away now. He hadn't wanted to kill anyone, not even Beatty. His flesh gripped him and shrank as if it had been plunged in acid. He gagged. He saw Beatty, a torch, not moving, fluttering out on the grass. He bit at his knuckles. I'm sorry, I'm sorry, oh God, sorry . . .

He tried to piece it all together, to go back to the normal pattern of life a few short days ago before the sieve and the sand, Denham's Dentifrice, moth voices, fireflies, the alarms and excursions, too much for a few short days, too much, indeed, for a lifetime.

Feet ran in the far end of the alley.

"Get up!" he told himself. "Dammit, get up!" he said to the leg, and stood. The pains were spikes driven in the kneecap and then only darning needles and then only common ordinary safety pins, and after he had shagged along fifty more hops and jumps, filling his hand with slivers from the board fence, the prickling was like someone blowing a spray of scalding water on that leg. And the leg was at last his own leg again. He had been afraid that running might break the loose ankle. Now, sucking all the night into his open mouth and blowing it out pale, with all the blackness left heavily inside himself, he set out in a steady jogging pace. He carried the books in his hands.

He thought of Faber.

Faber was back there in the steaming lump of tar that had no name or identity now. He had burnt Faber, too. He suddenly felt so shocked by this that he felt Faber was really dead, baked like a roach in that small green capsule shoved and lost in the pocket of a man who was now nothing but a frame skeleton strung with asphalt tendons.

You must remember, burn them or they'll burn you, he thought. Right now it's as simple as that.

He searched his pockets, the money was there, and in his other pocket he found the usual Seashell upon which the city was talking to itself in the cold black morning.

"Police Alert. Wanted: Fugitive in city. Has committed murder and crimes against the State. Name: Guy Montag. Occupation: Fireman. Last seen . . ."

He ran steadily for six blocks in the alley and then the alley opened out onto a wide empty thoroughfare ten lanes wide. It seemed like a boatless river frozen there in the raw light of the high white arc lamps; you could drown trying to cross it, he felt; it was too wide, it was too open. It was a vast stage without scenery, inviting him to run across, easily seen in the blazing illumination, easily caught, easily shot down.

The Seashell hummed in his ear.

". . . watch for a man running . . . watch for the running man . . . watch for a man alone, on foot . . . watch . . ."

Montag pulled back in the shadows. Directly ahead lay a gas station, a great chunk of porcelain snow shining there, and two silver beetles pulling in to fill up. Now he must be clean and presentable if he wished to walk, not run, stroll calmly across that wide boulevard. It would give him an extra margin of safety if he washed up and combed his hair before he went on his way to get *where?* . . .

Yes, he thought, where *am* I running?

Nowhere. There was nowhere to go, no friend to turn to, really. Except Faber. And then he realized that he was, indeed, running toward Faber's house, instinctively. But Faber couldn't hide him; it would be suicide even to try. But he knew that he would go to see Faber anyway, for a few short minutes. Faber's would be the place where he might refuel his fast-draining belief in his own ability to survive. He just wanted to know that there was a man like Faber in the world. He wanted to see the man alive and not burnt back there like a body shelled in another body. And some of the money must be left with Faber, of course, to be spent after Montag ran on his way. Perhaps he could make the open country and live on or near the rivers and near the highways, in the fields and hills.

A great whirling whisper made him look to the sky.

The police helicopters were rising so far away that it seemed someone had blown the gray head off a dry dandelion flower. Two dozen of them flurried, wavering, indecisive, three miles off, like butterflies puzzled by autumn, and then they were plummeting down to land, one by one, here, there, softly kneading the streets where, turned back to beetles, they shrieked along the boulevards or, as suddenly, leapt back into the air, continuing their search.

And here was the gas station, its attendants busy now with customers. Approaching from the rear, Montag entered the men's washroom. Through the aluminum wall he heard a radio voice saying, "War has been declared." The gas was being pumped outside. The men in the beetles were talking and the attendants were talking about the engines, the gas, the money owed. Montag stood trying to make himself feel the shock of the quiet statement from the radio, but nothing would happen. The war would have to wait for him to come to it in his personal file, an hour, two hours from now.

He washed his hands and face and toweled himself dry, making little sound. He came out of the washroom and shut the door carefully and walked into the darkness and at last stood again on the edge of the empty boulevard.

There it lay, a game for him to win, a vast bowling alley in the cool morning. The boulevard was as clean as the surface of an arena two minutes before the appearance of certain unnamed victims and certain unknown killers. The air over and above the vast concrete river trembled with the warmth of Montag's body alone; it was incredible how he felt his temperature could cause the whole immediate world to vibrate. He was a phosphorescent target; he knew it, he felt it. And now he must begin his little walk.

Three blocks away a few headlights glared. Montag drew a deep breath. His lungs were like burning brooms in his chest. His mouth was sucked dry from running. His throat tasted of bloody iron and there was rusted steel in his feet.

What about those lights there? Once you started walking you'd have to gauge how fast those beetles could make it down here. Well, how far was it to the other curb? It seemed like a hundred yards. Probably not a hundred, but figure for that anyway, figure that with him going very slowly, at a nice stroll, it might take as much as thirty seconds, forty seconds to walk all that way. The beetles? Once started, they could leave three blocks behind them in about fifteen seconds. So, even if halfway across he started to run . . . ?

He put his right foot out and then his left foot and then his right. He walked on the empty avenue.

Even if the street were entirely empty, of course, you couldn't be sure of a safe crossing, for a car could appear suddenly over the rise four blocks farther on and be on and past you before you had taken a dozen breaths.

He decided not to count his steps. He looked neither to left nor right. The light from the overhead lamps seemed as bright and revealing as the midday sun and just as hot.

He listened to the sound of the car picking up speed
two blocks away on his right. Its movable headlights
jerked back and forth suddenly, and caught at Montag.

Keep going.

Montag faltered, got a grip on the books, and
forced himself not to freeze. Instinctively he took
a few quick running steps, then talked out loud to
himself and pulled up to stroll again. He was now
half across the street, but the roar from the beetle's
engines whined higher as it put on speed.

The police, of course. They see me. But slow now
slow, quiet, don't turn, don't look, don't seem concerned. Walk, that's it, walk, walk.

The beetle was rushing. The beetle was roaring.
The beetle raised its speed. The beetle was whining.
The beetle was in high thunder. The beetle came
skimming. The beetle came in a single whistling trajectory, fired from an invisible rifle. It was up to 120
mph. It was up to 130 at least. Montag clamped his
jaws. The heat of the racing headlights burnt his
cheeks, it seemed, and jittered his eyelids and flushed
the sour sweat out all over his body.

He began to shuffle idiotically and talk to himself
and then he broke and just ran. He put out his legs
as far as they would go and down and then far out
again and down and back and out and down and
back. God! God! He dropped a book, broke pace,
almost turned, changed his mind, plunged on, yelling
in concrete emptiness, the beetle scuttling after its
running food, two hundred, one hundred feet away,
ninety, eighty, seventy, Montag gasping, flailing his
hands, legs up down out, up down out, closer,
closer, hooting, calling, his eyes burnt white now

as his head jerked about to confront the flashing
glare, now the beetle was swallowed in its own light,
now it was nothing but a torch hurtling upon him;
all sound, all blare. Now—almost on top of him!

He stumbled and fell.

I'm done! It's over!

But the falling made a difference. An instant before reaching him the wild beetle cut and swerved
out. It was gone. Montag lay flat, his head down.
Wisps of laughter trailed back to him with the blue
exhaust from the beetle.

His right hand was extended above him, flat.
Across the extreme tip of his middle finger, he saw
now as he lifted that hand, a faint sixteenth of an
inch of black tread where the tire had touched in
passing. He looked at that black line with disbelief,
getting to his feet.

That wasn't the police, he thought.

He looked down the boulevard. It was clear now.
A carful of children, all ages, God knew, from twelve
to sixteen, out whistling, yelling, hurrahing, had seen
a man, a very extraordinary sight, a man strolling, a
rarity, and simply said, "Let's get him," not knowing
he was the fugitive Mr. Montag, simply a number
of children out for a long night of roaring five or six
hundred miles in a few moonlit hours, their faces
icy with wind, and coming home or not coming at
dawn, alive or not alive, that made the adventure.

They would have killed me, thought Montag, swaying, the air still torn and stirring about him in dust,
touching his bruised cheek. For no reason at all in
the world they would have killed me.

He walked toward the far curb telling each foot
to go and keep going. Somehow he had picked up

the spilled books, he didn't remember bending or touching them. He kept moving them from hand to hand as if they were a poker hand he could not figure.

I wonder if they were the ones who killed Clarisse?

He stopped and his mind said it again, very loud.

I wonder if they were the ones who killed Clarisse!

He wanted to run after them yelling.

His eyes watered.

The thing that had saved him was falling flat. The driver of that car, seeing Montag down, instinctively considered the probability that running over a body at such a high speed might turn the car upside down and spill them out. If Montag had remained an *upright* target? . . .

Montag gasped.

Far down the boulevard, four blocks away, the beetle had slowed, spun about on two wheels, and was now racing back, slanting over on the wrong side of the street, picking up speed.

But Montag was gone, hidden in the safety of the dark alley for which he had set out on a long journey, an hour, or was it a minute, ago? He stood shivering in the night, looking back out as the beetle ran by and skidded back to the center of the avenue, whirling laughter in the air all about it, gone.

Farther on, as Montag moved in darkness, he could see the helicopters falling falling like the first flakes of snow in the long winter to come . . .

The house was silent.

Montag approached from the rear, creeping through a thick night-moistened scent of daffodils and roses and wet grass. He touched the screen door in back, found it open, slipped in, moved across the porch, listening.

Mrs. Black, are you asleep in there? he thought. This isn't good, but your husband did it to others and never asked and never wondered and never worried. And now since you're a fireman's wife, it's your house and your turn, for all the houses your husband burnt and the people he hurt without thinking.

The house did not reply.

He hid the books in the kitchen and moved from the house again to the alley and looked back and the house was still dark and quiet, sleeping.

On his way across town, with the helicopters fluttering like torn bits of paper in the sky, he phoned the alarm at a lonely phone booth outside a store that was closed for the night. Then he stood in the cold night air, waiting, and at a distance he heard the fire sirens start up and run, and the Salamanders coming, coming to burn Mr. Black's house while he was away at work, to make his wife stand shivering in the morning air while the roof let go and dropped in upon the fire. But now, she was still asleep.

Good night, Mrs. Black, he thought.

"Faber!"

Another rap, a whisper, and a long waiting. Then, after a minute, a small light flickered inside Faber's small house. After another pause, the back door opened.

They stood looking at each other in the half light, Faber and Montag, as if each did not believe in the other's existence. Then Faber moved and put out his hand and grabbed Montag and moved him in and sat

141

him down and went back and stood in the door, listening. The sirens were wailing off in the morning distance. He came in and shut the door.

Montag said, "I've been a fool all down the line. I can't stay long. I'm on my way God knows where."

"At least you were a fool about the right things," said Faber. "I thought you were dead. The audio-capsule I gave you—"

"Burnt."

"I heard the Captain talking to you and suddenly there was nothing. I almost came out looking for you."

"The Captain's dead. He found the audio-capsule, he heard your voice, he was going to trace it. I killed him with the flame thrower."

Faber sat down and did not speak for a time.

"My God, how did this happen?" said Montag. "It was only the other night everything was fine and the next thing I know I'm drowning. How many times can a man go down and still be alive? I can't breathe. There's Beatty dead, and he was my friend once, and there's Millie gone, I thought she was my wife, but now I don't know. And the house all burnt. And my job gone and myself on the run, and I planted a book in a fireman's house on the way. Good Christ, the things I've done in a single week!"

"You did what you had to do. It was coming on for a long time."

"Yes, I believe that, if there's nothing else I believe. It saved itself up to happen. I could feel it for a long time, I was saving something up, I went around doing one thing and feeling another. God, it was all there. It's a wonder it didn't show on me, like fat.

And now here I am, messing up your life, too. They might follow me here."

"I feel alive for the first time in years," said Faber. "I feel I'm doing what I should've done a lifetime ago. For a little while I'm not afraid. Maybe it's because I'm doing the right thing at last. Maybe it's because I've done a rash thing and don't want to look the coward to you. I suppose I'll have to do even more violent things, exposing myself so I won't fall down on the job and turn scared again. What are your plans?"

"To keep running."

"You know the war's on?"

"I heard."

"God, isn't it funny?" said the old man. "It seems so remote because we have our own troubles."

"I haven't had time to think." Montag drew out a hundred dollars. "I want this to stay with you. Use it any way that'll help when I'm gone."

"But—"

"I might be dead by noon; use this."

Faber nodded. "You'd better head for the river if you can, follow along it, and if you can hit the old railroad lines going out into the country, follow them. Even though practically everything's airborne these days and most of the tracks are abandoned, the rails are still there, rusting. I've heard there are still hobo camps all across the country, here and there; walking camps they call them, and if you keep walking far enough and keep an eye peeled, they say there's lots of old Harvard degrees on the tracks between here and Los Angeles. Most of them are wanted and hunted in the cities. They survive, I guess. There aren't many of them, and I guess the Govern-

ment's never considered them a great enough danger
to go in and track them down. You might hole up
with them for a time and get in touch with me in St.
Louis. I'm leaving on the five A.M. bus this morning,
to see a retired printer there. I'm getting out in the
open myself, at last. This money will be put to good
use. Thanks and God bless you. Do you want to
sleep a few minutes?"

"I'd better run."

"Let's check."

He took Montag quickly into the bedroom and
lifted a picture frame aside revealing a television
screen the size of a postal card. "I always wanted
something very small, something I could walk to,
something I could blot out with the palm of my
hand, if necessary, nothing that could shout me
down, nothing monstrous big. So, you see." He
snapped it on.

"Montag," the TV set said, and lit up. "M-O-N-
T-A-G." The name was spelled out by a voice. "Guy
Montag. Still running. Police helicopters are up. A
new Mechanical Hound has been brought from another district—"

Montag and Faber looked at each other.

"—Mechanical Hound *never* fails. Never since its
first use in tracking quarry has this incredible inven-
tion made a mistake. Tonight, this network is proud
to have the opportunity to follow the Hound by
camera helicopter as it starts on its way to the target—"

Faber poured two glasses of whiskey. "We'll need
these."

They drank.

"—nose so sensitive the Mechanical Hound can

remember and identify ten thousand odor indexes on ten thousand men without resetting!"

Faber trembled the least bit and looked about at his house, at the walls, the door, the doorknob, and the chair where Montag now sat. Montag saw the look. They both looked quickly about the house and Montag felt his nostrils dilate and he knew that he was trying to track himself and his nose was suddenly good enough to sense the path he had made in the air of the room and the sweat of his hand hung from the doorknob, invisible but as numerous as the jewels of a small chandelier, he was a luminous cloud, a ghost that made breathing once more impossible. He saw Faber stop up his own breath for fear of drawing that ghost into his own body, perhaps, being contaminated with the phantom exhalations and odors of a running man.

"The Mechanical Hound is now landing by helicopter at the site of the Burning!"

And there on the small screen was the burnt house, and the crowd and something with a sheet over it and out of the sky, fluttering, came the helicopter like a grotesque flower.

So they must have their game out, thought Montag. The circus must go on, even with war beginning within the hour . . .

He watched the scene, fascinated, not wanting to move. It seemed so remote and no part of him; it was a play apart and separate, wondrous to watch, not without its strange pleasure. That's all for me, he thought, that's all taking place just for *me*, by God.

If he wished, he could linger here, in comfort, and follow the entire hunt on through its swift phases, down alleys, across streets, over empty running ave-

nues, crossing lots and playgrounds, with pauses here
or there for the necessary commercials, up other
alleys to the burning house of Mr. and Mrs. Black,
and so on finally to this house with Faber and himself seated, drinking, while the Electric Hound
snuffed down the last trail, silent as a drift of death
itself, skidding to a halt outside that window there.
Then, if he wished, Montag might rise, walk to the
window, keep one eye on the TV screen, open the
window, lean out, look back, and see himself dra-
matized, described, made over, standing there, limned
in the bright small television screen from outside, a
drama to be watched objectively, knowing that in
other parlors he was large as life, in full color,
dimensionally perfect! and if he kept his eye peeled
quickly he would see himself, an instant before oblivion, being punctured for the benefit of how many
civilian parlor-sitters who had been wakened from
sleep a few minutes ago by the frantic sirening of
their living room walls to come watch the big game,
the hunt, the one-man carnival.

Would he have time for a speech? As the Hound
seized him, in view of ten or twenty or thirty million
people, mightn't he sum up his entire life in the last
week in one single phrase or a word that would stay
with them long after the Hound had turned, clenching him in its metal-plier jaws, and trotted off in
darkness, while the camera remained stationary,
watching the creature dwindle in the distance, a
splendid fade-out! What could he say in a single
word, a few words, that would sear all their faces
and wake them up?

"There," whispered Faber.

Out of a helicopter glided something that was not

machine, not animal, not dead, not alive, glowing
with a pale green luminosity. It stood near the smoking ruins of Montag's house and the men brought his
discarded flame thrower to it and put it down under
the muzzle of the Hound. There was a whirring,
clicking, humming.

Montag shook his head and got up and drank the
rest of his drink. "It's time. I'm sorry about this."

"About what? Me? My house? I deserve everything. Run, for God's sake. Perhaps I can delay them
here—"

"Wait. There's no use you being discovered. When
I leave, burn the spread of this bed that I touched.
Burn the chair in the living room in your wall incinerator. Wipe down the furniture with alcohol,
wipe the doorknobs. Burn the throw rug in the parlor. Turn the air-conditioning on full in all the rooms
and spray with moth spray if you have it. Then, turn
on your lawn sprinklers as high as they'll go and
hose off the sidewalks. With any luck at all, we can
kill the trail *in* here, anyway."

Faber shook his hand. "I'll tend to it. Good luck.
If we're both in good health, next week, the week
after, get in touch, General Delivery, St. Louis. I'm
sorry there's no way I can go with you this time by
earphone. That was good for both of us. But my
equipment was limited. You see, I never thought I
would use it. What a silly old man. No thought there.
Stupid, stupid. So I haven't another green bullet, the
right kind, to put in your head. Go now!"

"One last thing. Quick. A suitcase, get it, fill it
with your dirtiest clothes, an old suit, the dirtier the
better, a shirt, some old sneakers and socks . . ."

Faber was gone and back in a minute. They sealed

the cardboard valise with clear tape. "To keep the ancient odor of Mr. Faber in, of course," said Faber, sweating at the job.

Montag doused the exterior of the valise with whiskey. "I don't want that Hound picking up two odors at once. May I take this whiskey? I'll need it later. Christ, I hope this works!"

They shook hands again and going out the door glanced at the TV. The Hound was on its way, followed by hovering helicopter cameras, silently, silently, sniffing the great night wind. It was running down the first alley.

"Good-bye!"

And Montag was out the back door lightly, running with the half-empty valise. Behind him he heard the lawn sprinkling system jump up, filling the dark air with rain that fell gently and then with a steady pour all about, washing on the sidewalks and draining into the alley. He carried a few drops of this rain with him on his face. He thought he heard the old man call good-bye, but he wasn't certain.

He ran very fast away from the house, down toward the river.

Montag ran.

He could feel the Hound, like autumn, come cold and dry and swift, like a wind that didn't stir grass, that didn't jar windows or disturb leaf shadows on the white sidewalks as it passed. The Hound did not touch the world. It carried its silence with it, so you could feel the silence building up a pressure behind you all across town. Montag felt the pressure rising, and ran.

He stopped for breath, on his way to the river,

to peer through dimly lit windows of wakened houses, and saw the silhouettes of people inside watching their parlor walls and there on the walls the Mechanical Hound, a breath of neon vapor, spidered along, here and gone, here and gone! Now at Elm Terrace, Lincoln, Oak, Park, and up the alley toward Faber's house!

Go past, thought Montag, don't stop, go on, don't turn in!

On the parlor wall, Faber's house, with its sprinkler system pulsing in the night air.

The Hound paused, quivering.

No! Montag held to the windowsill. This way! *Here!*

The procaine needle flicked out and in, out and in. A single clear drop of the stuff of dreams fell from the needle as it vanished in the Hound's muzzle.

Montag held his breath, like a doubled fist, in his chest.

The Mechanical Hound turned and plunged away from Faber's house down the alley again.

Montag snapped his gaze to the sky. The helicopters were closer, a great blowing of insects to a single light source.

With an effort, Montag reminded himself again that this was no fictional episode to be watched on his run to the river; it was in actuality his own chess game he was witnessing, move by move.

He shouted to give himself the necessary push away from this last house window, and the fascinating seance going on in there. *Hell!* and he was away and gone! The alley, a street, the alley, a street, and the smell of the river. Leg out, leg down, leg out and down. Twenty million Montags running, soon, if the cameras caught him. Twenty million Montags running, running like an ancient flickery Keystone Comedy, cops, robbers, chasers and the chased, hunters and hunted, he had seen it a thousand times. Behind him now twenty million silently baying Hounds, ricocheted across parlors, three-cushion shooting from right wall to center wall to left wall, gone, right wall, center wall, left wall, gone!

Montag jammed his Seashell to his ear:

"Police suggest entire population in the Elm Terrace area do as follows: Everyone in every house in every street open a front or rear door or look from the windows. The fugitive cannot escape if everyone in the next minute looks from his house. Ready!"

Of course! Why hadn't they done it before! Why, in all the years, hadn't this game been tried! Everyone up, everyone out! He couldn't be missed! The only man running alone in the night city, the only man proving his legs!

"At the count of ten now! *One! Two!*"

He felt the city rise.

"Three!"

He felt the city turn to its thousands of doors.

Faster! Leg up, leg down!

"Four!"

The people sleepwalking in their hallways.

"Five!"

He felt their hands on the doorknobs!

The smell of the river was cool and like a solid rain. His throat was burnt rust and his eyes were wept dry with running. He yelled as if this yell would jet him on, fling him the last hundred yards.

"Six, seven, eight!"

The doorknobs turned on five thousand doors.

"Nine!"

He ran out away from the last row of houses, on a slope leading down to a solid, moving blackness.

"Ten!"

The doors opened.

He imagined thousands on thousands of faces peering into yards, into alleys, and into the sky, faces hid by curtains, pale, night-frightened faces, like gray animals peering from electric caves, faces with gray colorless eyes, gray tongues, and gray thoughts looking out through the numb flesh of the face.

But he was at the river.

He touched it, just to be sure it was real. He waded in and stripped in darkness to the skin, splashed his body, arms, legs, and head with raw liquor; drank it and snuffed some up his nose. Then he dressed in Faber's old clothes and shoes. He tossed his own clothing into the river and watched it swept away. Then, holding the suitcase, he walked out in the river until there was no bottom and he was swept away in the dark.

He was three hundred yards downstream when the Hound reached the river. Overhead the great racketing fans of the helicopters hovered. A storm of light fell upon the river and Montag dived under the great illumination as if the sun had broken the clouds. He felt the river pull him farther on its way, into darkness. Then the lights switched back to the land, the helicopters swerved over the city again, as if they had picked up another trail. They were gone. The Hound was gone. Now there was only the cold river and Montag floating in a sudden peacefulness, away from the city and the lights and the chase, away from everything.

He felt as if he had left a stage behind and many actors. He felt as if he had left the great seance and all the murmuring ghosts. He was moving from an unreality that was frightening into a reality that was unreal because it was new.

The black land slid by and he was going into the country among the hills. For the first time in a dozen years the stars were coming out above him, in great processions of wheeling fire. He saw a great juggernaut of stars form in the sky and threaten to roll over and crush him.

He floated on his back when the valise filled and sank; the river was mild and leisurely, going away from the people who ate shadows for breakfast and steam for lunch and vapors for supper. The river was very real; it held him comfortably and gave him the time at last, the leisure, to consider this month, this year, and a lifetime of years. He listened to his heart slow. His thoughts stopped rushing with his blood.

He saw the moon low in the sky now. The moon there, and the light of the moon caused by what? By the sun, of course. And what lights the sun? Its own fire. And the sun goes on, day after day, burning and burning. The sun and time. The sun and time and burning. Burning. The river bobbled him along gently. Burning. The sun and every clock on the earth. It all came together and became a single thing in his mind. After a long time of floating on the land and a short time of floating in the river he knew why he must never burn again in his life.

The sun burnt every day. It burnt Time. The world rushed in a circle and turned on its axis and time was busy burning the years and the people anyway, without any help from him. So if *he* burnt things with the firemen and the sun burnt Time, that meant that *everything* burnt!

One of them had to stop burning. The sun wouldn't, certainly. So it looked as if it had to be Montag and the people he had worked with until a few short hours ago. Somewhere the saving and putting away had to begin again and someone had to do the saving and keeping, one way or another, in books, in records, in people's heads, any way at all so long as it was safe, free from moths, silverfish, rust and dry-rot, and men with matches. The world was full of burning of all types and sizes. Now the guild of the asbestos weaver must open shop very soon.

He felt his heel bump land, touch pebbles and rocks, scrape sand. The river had moved him toward shore.

He looked in at the great black creature without eyes or light, without shape, with only a size that went a thousand miles, without wanting to stop, with its grass hills and forests that were waiting for him.

He hesitated to leave the comforting flow of the water. He expected the Hound there. Suddenly the trees might blow under a great wind of helicopters.

But there was only the normal autumn wind high up, going by like another river. Why wasn't the Hound running? Why had the search veered inland? Montag *listened*. Nothing. Nothing.

Millie, he thought. All this country here. Listen to it! Nothing and nothing. So much silence, Millie, I wonder how you'd take it? Would you shout, Shut up, shut up! Millie, Millie. And he was sad.

Millie was not here and the Hound was not here, but the dry smell of hay blowing from some distant field put Montag on the land. He remembered a farm he had visited when he was very young, one of the rare few times he discovered that somewhere behind the seven veils of unreality, beyond the walls of parlors and beyond the tin moat of the city, cows chewed grass and pigs sat in warm ponds at noon and dogs barked after white sheep on a hill.

Now the dry smell of hay, the motion of the waters, made him think of sleeping in fresh hay in a lonely barn away from the loud highways, behind a quiet farmhouse, and under an ancient windmill that whirred like the sound of the passing years overhead. He lay in the high barn loft all night, listening to distant animals and insects and trees, the little motions and stirrings.

During the night, he thought, below the loft, he would hear a sound like feet moving, perhaps. He would tense and sit up. The sound would move away. He would lie back and look out the loft window, very late in the night, and see the lights go out in the farmhouse itself, until a very young and beautiful woman would sit in an unlit window, braiding her hair. It would be hard to see her, but her face would be like the face of the girl so long ago in his past now, so very long ago, the girl who had known the weather and never been burnt by the fireflies, the girl who had known what dandelions meant rubbed off on your chin. Then, she would be gone from the warm window and appear again upstairs in her moon-whitened room. And then, to the sound of death, the sound of the jets cutting the sky in two black pieces beyond the horizon, he would lie in the loft, hidden and safe, watching those strange new stars over the rim of the earth, fleeing from the soft color of dawn.

In the morning he would not have needed sleep, for all the warm odors and sights of a complete country night would have rested and slept him while his eyes were wide and his mouth, when he thought to test it, was half a smile.

And there at the bottom of the hayloft stair waiting for him would be the incredible thing. He would step carefully down, in the pink light of early morning, so fully aware of the world that he would be afraid, and stand over the small miracle and at last bend to touch it.

A cool glass of fresh milk, and a few apples and pears laid at the foot of the steps.

This was all he wanted now. Some sign that the immense world would accept him and give him the long time he needed to think all the things that must be thought.

A glass of milk, an apple, a pear.

He stepped from the river.

The land rushed at him, a tidal wave. He was crushed by darkness and the look of the country and the million odors on a wind that iced his body. He fell back under the breaking curve of darkness and sound and smell, his ears roaring. He whirled. The stars poured over his sight like flaming meteors. He wanted to plunge in the river again and let it idle him safely on down somewhere. This dark land rising was like that day in his childhood, swimming, when from nowhere the largest wave in the history of remembering slammed him down in salt mud and green darkness, water burning mouth and nose, retching his stomach, screaming! Too much water!

Too much land.

Out of the black wall before him, a whisper. A shape. In the shape, two eyes. The night looking at him. The forest, seeing him.

The Hound!

After all the running and rushing and sweating it out and half drowning, to come this far, work this hard, and think yourself safe and sigh with relief and come out on the land at last only to find . . .

The Hound!

Montag gave one last agonized shout as if this were too much for any man.

The shape exploded away. The eyes vanished. The leaf piles flew up in a dry shower.

Montag was alone in the wilderness.

A deer. He smelled the heavy musk like perfume mingled with blood and the gummed exhalation of the animal's breath, all cardamom and moss and ragweed odor in this huge night where the trees ran at him, pulled away, ran, pulled away, to the pulse of the heart behind his eyes.

There must have been a billion leaves on the land; he waded in them, a dry river smelling of hot cloves and warm dust. And the other smells! There was a smell like a cut potato from all the land, raw and cold and white from having the moon on it most of the night. There was a smell like pickles from a bottle and a smell like parsley on the table at home. There was a faint yellow odor like mustard from a jar. There was a smell like carnations from the yard next door. He put down his hand and felt a weed rise up like a child brushing him. His fingers smelled of licorice.

He stood breathing, and the more he breathed the land in, the more he was filled up with all the details of the land. He was not empty. There was more than enough here to fill him. There would always be more than enough.

He walked in the shallow tide of leaves, stumbling.

And in the middle of the strangeness, a familiarity.

His foot hit something that rang dully.

He moved his hand on the ground, a yard this way, a yard that.

The railroad track.

The track that came out of the city and rusted across the land, through forests and woods, deserted now, by the river.

Here was the path to wherever he was going. Here was the single familiar thing, the magic charm he might need a little while, to touch, to feel beneath his feet, as he moved on into the bramble bushes and the lakes of smelling and feeling and touching, among the whispers and the blowing down of leaves.

He walked on the track.

And he was surprised to learn how certain he suddenly was of a single fact he could not prove.

Once, long ago, Clarisse had walked here, where he was walking now.

Half an hour later, cold, and moving carefully on the tracks, fully aware of his entire body, his face, his mouth, his eyes stuffed with blackness, his ears stuffed with sound, his legs prickled with burrs and nettles, he saw the fire ahead.

The fire was gone, then back again, like a winking

eye. He stopped, afraid he might blow the fire out with a single breath. But the fire was there and he approached warily, from a long way off. It took the better part of fifteen minutes before he drew very close indeed to it, and then he stood looking at it from cover. That small motion, the white and red color, a strange fire because it meant a different thing to him.

It was not burning. It was *warming*.

He saw many hands held to its warmth, hands without arms, hidden in darkness. Above the hands, motionless faces that were only moved and tossed and flickered with firelight. He hadn't known fire could look this way. He had never thought in his life that it could give as well as take. Even its smell was different.

How long he stood he did not know, but there was a foolish and yet delicious sense of knowing himself as an animal come from the forest, drawn by the fire. He was a thing of brush and liquid eye, of fur and muzzle and hoof, he was a thing of horn and blood that would smell like autumn if you bled it out on the ground. He stood a long long time, listening to the warm crackle of the flames.

There was a silence gathered all about that fire and the silence was in the men's faces, and time was there, time enough to sit by this rusting track under the trees and look at the world and turn it over with the eyes, as if it were held to the center of the bonfire, a piece of steel these men were all shaping. It was not only the fire that was different. It was the silence. Montag moved toward this special silence that was concerned with all of the world.

And then the voices began and they were talking,

and he could hear nothing of what the voices said, but the sound rose and fell quietly and the voices were turning the world over and looking at it; the voices knew the land and the trees and the city which lay down the track by the river. The voices talked of everything, there was nothing they could not talk about, he knew, from the very cadence and motion and continual stir of curiosity and wonder in them.

And then one of the men looked up and saw him, for the first or perhaps the seventh time, and a voice called to Montag:

"All right, you can come out now!"

Montag stepped back in the shadows.

"It's all right," the voice said. "You're welcome here."

Montag walked slowly toward the fire and the five old men sitting there dressed in the dark-blue denim pants and jackets and dark-blue shirts. He did not know what to say to them.

"Sit down," said the man who seemed to be the leader of the small group. "Have some coffee?"

He watched the dark steaming mixture pour into a collapsible tin cup, which was handed him straight off. He sipped it gingerly and felt them looking at him with curiosity. His lips were scalded, but that was good. The faces around him were bearded, but the beards were clean, neat, and their hands were clean. They had stood up as if to welcome a guest, and now they sat down again. Montag sipped. "Thanks," he said. "Thanks very much."

"You're welcome, Montag. My name's Granger." He held out a small bottle of colorless fluid. "Drink this, too. It'll change the chemical index of your perspiration. Half an hour from now you'll smell like two other people. With the Hound after you, the best thing is bottoms up."

Montag drank the bitter fluid.

"You'll stink like a bobcat, but that's all right," said Granger.

"You know my name," said Montag.

Granger nodded to a portable battery TV set by the fire. "We've watched the chase. Figured you'd wind up south along the river. When we heard you plunging around out in the forest like a drunken elk, we didn't hide as we usually do. We figured you were in the river, when the helicopter cameras swung back in over the city. Something funny there. The chase is still running. The other way, though."

"The other way?"

"Let's have a look."

Granger snapped the portable viewer on. The picture was a nightmare, condensed, easily passed from hand to hand in the forest, all whirring color and flight. A voice cried:

"The chase continues north in the city! Police helicopters are converging on Avenue 87 and Elm Grove Park!"

Granger nodded. "They're faking. You threw them off at the river. They can't admit it. They know they can hold their audience only so long. The show's got to have a snap ending, quick! If they started searching the whole damn river it might take all night. So they're sniffing for a scapegoat to end things with a bang. Watch. They'll catch Montag in the next five minutes!"

"But how—"

"Watch."

The camera, hovering in the belly of a helicopter, now swung down at an empty street.

"See that?" whispered Granger. "It'll be you; right up at the end of that street is our victim. See how our camera is coming in? Building the scene. Suspense. Long shot. Right now, some poor fellow is out for a walk. A rarity. An odd one. Don't think the police don't know the habits of queer ducks like that, men who walk mornings for the hell of it, or for reasons of insomnia. Anyway, the police have had him charted for months, years. Never know when that sort of information might be handy. And today, it turns out, it's very usable indeed. It saves face. Oh God, look there!"

The men at the fire bent forward.

On the screen, a man turned a corner. The Mechanical Hound rushed forward into the viewer, suddenly. The helicopter lights shot down a dozen brilliant pillars that built a cage all about the man.

A voice cried, "There's Montag! The search is *done.*"

The innocent man stood bewildered, a cigarette burning in his hand. He stared at the Hound, not knowing what it was. He probably never knew. He glanced up at the sky and the wailing sirens. The camera rushed down. The Hound leapt up into the air with a rhythm and a sense of timing that was incredibly beautiful. Its needle shot out. It was suspended for a moment in their gaze, as if to give the vast audience time to appreciate everything, the raw look of the victim's face, the empty street, the steel animal a bullet nosing the target.

"Montag, don't move!" said a voice from the sky.

The camera fell upon the victim, even as did the

Hound. Both reached him simultaneously. The victim was seized by Hound and camera in a great spidering, clenching grip. He screamed. He screamed. He screamed!

Blackout.

Silence.

Darkness.

Montag cried out in the silence and turned away.

Silence.

And then, after a time of the men sitting around the fire, their faces expressionless, an announcer on the dark screen said, "The search is over, Montag is dead; a crime against society has been avenged."

Darkness.

"We now take you to the Sky Room of the Hotel Lux for a half hour of Just-Before-Dawn, a program of—"

Granger turned it off.

"They didn't show the man's face in focus. Did you notice? Even your best friends couldn't tell if it was you. They scrambled it just enough to let the imagination take over. Hell," he whispered. "Hell."

Montag said nothing but now, looking back, sat with his eyes fixed to the blank screen, trembling.

Granger touched Montag's arm. "Welcome back from the dead." Montag nodded. Granger went on. "You might as well know all of us, now. This is Fred Clement, former occupant of the Thomas Hardy chair at Cambridge in the years before it became an Atomic Engineering School. This other is Dr. Simmons from U. C. L. A., a specialist in Ortega y Gasset; Professor West here did quite a bit for ethics, an ancient study now, for Columbia University quite some years ago. Reverend Padover here gave a few lectures thirty years ago and lost his flock between one Sunday and the next for his views. He's been bumming with us some time now. Myself: I wrote a book called *The Fingers in the Glove; the Proper Relationship between the Individual and Society,* and here I *am!* Welcome, Montag!"

"I don't belong with you," said Montag, at last, slowly. "I've been an idiot all the way."

"We're used to that. We all made the *right* kind of mistakes, or we wouldn't be here. When we were separate individuals, all we had was rage. I struck a fireman when he came to burn my library years ago. I've been running ever since. You want to join us, Montag?"

"Yes."

"What have you to offer?"

"Nothing. I thought I had part of the Book of Ecclesiastes and maybe a little of Revelation, but I haven't even that now."

"The Book of Ecclesiastes would be fine. Where was it?"

"Here." Montag touched his head.

"Ah." Granger smiled and nodded.

"What's wrong? Isn't that all right?" said Montag.

"Better than all right; perfect!" Granger turned to the Reverend. "Do we have a Book of Ecclesiastes?"

"One. A man named Harris in Youngstown."

"Montag." Granger took Montag's shoulder firmly. "Walk carefully. Guard your health. If anything should happen to Harris, *you* are the Book of Ecclesiastes. See how important you've become in the last minute!"

"But I've forgotten!"

"No, nothing's ever lost. We have ways to shake down your clinkers for you."

"But I've tried to remember!"

"Don't try. It'll come when we need it. All of us have photographic memories, but spend a lifetime learning how to block off the things that are really *in* there. Simmons here has worked on it for twenty years and now we've got the method down to where we can recall anything that's been read once. Would you like, someday, Montag, to read Plato's *Republic*?"

"Of course!"

"*I* am Plato's *Republic*. Like to read Marcus Aurelius? Mr. Simmons is Marcus."

"How do you do?" said Mr. Simmons.

"Hello," said Montag.

"I want you to meet Jonathan Swift, the author of that evil political book, *Gulliver's Travels!* And this other fellow is Charles Darwin, and this one is Schopenhauer, and this one is Einstein, and this one here at my elbow is Mr. Albert Schweitzer, a very kind philosopher indeed. Here we all are, Montag. Aristophanes and Mahatma Gandhi and Gautama Buddha and Confucius and Thomas Love Peacock and Thomas Jefferson and Mr. Lincoln, if you please. We are also Matthew, Mark, Luke, and John."

Everyone laughed quietly.

"It can't *be*," said Montag.

"It *is*," replied Granger, smiling. "*We're* book burners, too. We read the books and burnt them, afraid they'd be found. Microfilming didn't pay off; we were always traveling, we didn't want to bury the film and come back later. Always the chance of discovery. Better to keep it in the old heads, where no one can see it or suspect it. We are all bits and pieces of history and literature and international law. Byron, Tom Paine, Machiavelli, or Christ, it's here. And the hour's late. And the war's begun. And we are out here, and the city is there, all wrapped up in its own coat of a thousand colors. What do you think, Montag?"

"I think I was blind trying to go at things my way, planting books in firemen's houses and sending in alarms."

"You did what you had to do. Carried out on a national scale, it might have worked beautifully. But our way is simpler and, we think, better. All we want to do is keep the knowledge we think we will need intact and safe. We're not out to incite or anger anyone yet. For if we are destroyed, the knowledge is dead, perhaps for good. We are model citizens, in our own special way; we walk the old tracks, we lie in the hills at night, and the city people let us be. We're stopped and searched occasionally, but there's nothing on our persons to incriminate us. The organization is flexible, very loose, and fragmentary. Some of us have had plastic surgery on our faces and fingerprints. Right now we have a horrible job; we're waiting for the war to begin and, as quickly, end. It's not pleasant, but then we're not in control, we're the odd minority crying in the wilderness. When the war's over, perhaps we can be of some use in the world."

"Do you really think they'll listen then?"

"If not, we'll just have to wait. We'll pass the books on to our children, by word of mouth, and let our children wait, in turn, on the other people. A lot will be lost that way, of course. But you can't *make*

165

people listen. They have to come 'round in their own time, wondering what happened and why the world blew up under them. It can't last."

"How many of you are there?"

"Thousands on the roads, the abandoned rail-tracks, tonight, bums on the outside, libraries inside. It wasn't planned, at first. Each man had a book he wanted to remember, and did. Then, over a period of twenty years or so, we met each other, traveling, and got the loose network together and set out a plan. The most important single thing we had to pound into ourselves is that we were not important, we mustn't be pedants; we were not to feel superior to anyone else in the world. We're nothing more than dust jackets for books, of no significance otherwise. Some of us live in small towns. Chapter One of Thoreau's *Walden* in Green River, Chapter Two in Willow Farm, Maine. Why, there's one town in Maryland, only twenty-seven people, no bomb'll ever touch that town, is the complete essays of a man named Bertrand Russell. Pick up that town, almost, and flip the pages, so many pages to a person. And when the war's over, someday, some year, the books can be written again, the people will be called in, one by one, to recite what they know and we'll set it up in type until another Dark Age, when we might have to do the whole damn thing over again. But that's the wonderful thing about man; he never gets so discouraged or disgusted that he gives up doing it all over again, because he knows very well it is important and *worth* the doing."

"What do we do tonight?" asked Montag.

"Wait," said Granger. "And move downstream a little ways, just in case."

He began throwing dust and dirt in the fire.

The other men helped, and Montag helped, and there, in the wilderness, the men all moved their hands, putting out the fire together.

They stood by the river in the starlight.

Montag saw the luminous dial of his waterproof watch. Five. Five o'clock in the morning. Another year ticked by in a single hour, and dawn waiting beyond the far bank of the river.

"Why do you trust me?" said Montag.

A man moved in the darkness.

"The look of you's enough. You haven't seen yourself in a mirror lately. Beyond that, the city has never cared so much about us to bother with an elaborate chase like this to find us. A few crackpots with verses in their heads can't touch them, and they know it and we know it; everyone knows it. So long as the vast population doesn't wander about quoting the Magna Carta and the Constitution, it's all right. The firemen were enough to check that, now and then. No, the cities don't bother us. And *you* look like hell."

They moved along the bank of the river, going south. Montag tried to see the men's faces, the old faces he remembered from the firelight, lined and tired. He was looking for a brightness, a resolve, a triumph over tomorrow that hardly seemed to be there. Perhaps he had expected their faces to burn and glitter with the knowledge they carried, to glow as lanterns glow, with the light in them. But all the light had come from the campfire, and these men had seemed no different than any others who had run a long race, searched a long search, seen good things destroyed, and now, very late, were gathered to wait for the end of the party and the blowing out of the lamps. They weren't at all certain that the things they carried in their heads might make every future dawn glow with a purer light, they were sure of nothing save that the books were on file behind their quiet eyes, the books were waiting, with their pages uncut, for the customers who might come by in later years, some with clean and some with dirty fingers.

Montag squinted from one face to another as they walked.

"Don't judge a book by its cover," someone said.

And they all laughed quietly, moving downstream.

There was a shriek and the jets from the city were gone overhead long before the men looked up. Montag stared back at the city, far down the river, only a faint glow now.

"My wife's back there."

"I'm sorry to hear that. The cities won't do well in the next few days," said Granger.

"It's strange, I don't miss her, it's strange I don't feel much of anything," said Montag. "Even if she dies, I realized a moment ago, I don't think I'll feel sad. It isn't right. Something must be wrong with me."

"Listen," said Granger, taking his arm and walking with him, holding aside the bushes to let him pass. "When I was a boy my grandfather died, and he was a sculptor. He was also a very kind man who had a lot of love to give the world, and he helped clean up the slum in our town; and he made toys for us and he did a million things in his lifetime;

he was always busy with his hands. And when he died, I suddenly realized I wasn't crying for him at all, but for all the things he did. I cried because he would never do them again, he would never carve another piece of wood or help us raise doves and pigeons in the backyard or play the violin the way he did, or tell us jokes the way he did. He was part of us and when he died, all the actions stopped dead and there was no one to do them just the way he did. He was individual. He was an important man. I've never gotten over his death. Often I think what wonderful carvings never came to birth because he died. How many jokes are missing from the world, and how many homing pigeons untouched by his hands. He shaped the world. He *did* things to the world. The world was bankrupted of ten million fine actions the night he passed on."

Montag walked in silence. "Millie, Millie," he whispered. "Millie."

"What?"

"My wife, my wife. Poor Millie, poor, poor Millie. I can't remember anything. I think of her hands but I don't see them doing anything at all. They just hang there at her sides or they lay there on her lap or there's a cigarette in them, but that's all."

Montag turned and glanced back.

What did you give to the city, Montag?

Ashes.

What did the others give to each other?

Nothingness.

Granger stood looking back with Montag. "Everyone must leave something behind when he dies, my grandfather said. A child or a book or a painting or a house or a wall built or a pair of shoes made. Or a garden planted. Something your hand touched some way so your soul has somewhere to go when you die, and when people look at that tree or that flower you planted, you're there. It doesn't matter what you do, he said, so long as you change something from the way it was before you touched it into something that's like you after you take your hands away. The difference between the man who just cuts lawns and a real gardener is in the touching, he said. The lawn cutter might just as well not have been there at all; the gardener will be there a lifetime."

Granger moved his hand. "My grandfather showed me some V-2 rocket films once, fifty years ago. Have you ever seen the atom-bomb mushroom from two hundred miles up? It's a pinprick, it's nothing. With the wilderness all around it.

"My grandfather ran off the V-2 rocket film a dozen times and then hoped that someday our cities would open up more and let the green and the land and the wilderness in more, to remind people that we're allotted a little space on earth and that we survive in that wilderness that can take back what it has given, as easily as blowing its breath on us or sending the sea to tell us we are not so big. When we forget how close the wilderness is in the night, my grandpa said, someday it will come in and get us, for we will have forgotten how terrible and real it can be. You see?" Granger turned to Montag. "Grandfather's been dead for all these years, but if you lifted my skull, by God, in the convolutions of my brain you'd find the big ridges of his thumbprint. He touched me. As I said earlier, he was a sculptor. 'I hate a Roman named Status Quo!' he said to me. 'Stuff your eyes with wonder,' he said, 'live as if you'd drop dead in ten seconds. See the world. It's more fantastic than any dream made or paid for in factories. Ask no guarantees, ask for no security, there never was such an animal. And if there were, it would be related to the great sloth which hangs upside down in a tree all day every day, sleeping its life away. To hell with that,' he said, 'shake the tree and knock the great sloth down on his ass.'"

"Look!" cried Montag.

And the war began and ended in that instant.

Later, the men around Montag could not say if they had really seen anything. Perhaps the merest flourish of light and motion in the sky. Perhaps the bombs were there, and the jets, ten miles, five miles, one mile up, for the merest instant, like grain thrown over the heavens by a great sowing hand, and the bombs drifting with dreadful swiftness, yet sudden slowness, down upon the morning city they had left behind. The bombardment was to all intents and purposes finished once the jets had sighted their target, alerted their bombardier at five thousand miles an hour; as quick as the whisper of a scythe the war was finished. Once the bomb release was yanked, it was over. Now, a full three seconds, all of the time in history, before the bombs struck, the enemy ships themselves were gone half around the visible world, like bullets in which a savage islander might not believe because they were invisible; yet the heart is suddenly shattered, the body falls in separate motions, and the blood is astonished to be freed on the air; the brain squanders its few precious memories and, puzzled, dies.

This was not to be believed. It was merely a gesture. Montag saw the flirt of a great metal fist over the far city and he knew the scream of the jets that would follow, would say, after the deed, *disintegrate, leave no stone on another, perish. Die.*

Montag held the bombs in the sky for a single moment, with his mind and his hands reaching helplessly up at them. "Run!" he cried to Faber. To Clarisse, "Run!" To Mildred, "Get out, get out of there!" But Clarisse, he remembered, was dead. And Faber *was* out; there in the deep valleys of the country somewhere the five A.M. bus was on its way from one desolation to another. Though the desolation had not yet arrived, was still in the air, it was certain as man could make it. Before the bus had run another fifty yards on the highway, its destination would be meaningless, and its point of departure changed from metropolis to junkyard.

And Mildred . . .

Get out, run!

He saw her in her hotel room somewhere now in the half second remaining with the bombs a yard, a foot, an inch from her building. He saw her leaning toward the great shimmering walls of color and motion where the family talked and talked and talked to her, where the family prattled and chatted and said her name and smiled at her and said nothing of the bomb that was an inch, now a half inch, now a quarter inch from the top of the hotel. Leaning into the wall as if all of the hunger of looking would find the secret of her sleepless unease there. Mildred, leaning anxiously, nervously, as if to plunge, drop, fall into that swarming immensity of color to drown in its bright happiness.

The first bomb struck.

"Mildred!"

172

Perhaps, who would ever know? perhaps the great broadcasting stations with their beams of color and light and talk and chatter went first into oblivion.

Montag, falling flat, going down, saw or felt, or imagined he saw or felt the walls go dark in Millie's face, heard her screaming, because in the millionth part of time left, she saw her own face reflected there, in a mirror instead of a crystal ball, and it was such a wildly empty face, all by itself in the room, touching nothing, starved and eating of itself, that at last she recognized it as her own and looked quickly up at the ceiling as it and the entire structure of the hotel blasted down upon her, carrying her with a million pounds of brick, metal, plaster, and wood, to meet other people in the hives below, all on their quick way down to the cellar where the explosion rid itself of them in its own unreasonable way.

I remember. Montag clung to the earth. I remember. Chicago. Chicago a long time ago. Millie and I. *That's* where we met! I remember now. Chicago. A long time ago.

The concussion knocked the air across and down the river, turned the men over like dominos in a line, blew the water in lifting sprays, and blew the dust and made the trees above them mourn with a great wind passing away south. Montag crushed himself down, squeezing himself small, eyes tight. He blinked once. And in that instant saw the city, instead of the bombs, in the air. They had displaced each other. For another of those impossible instants the city stood, rebuilt and unrecognizable, taller than it had ever hoped or strived to be, taller than man had built it, erected at last in grouts of shattered concrete and sparkles of torn metal into a mural hung like a reversed avalanche, a million colors, a million oddities, a door where a window should be, a top for a bottom, a side for a back, and then the city rolled over and fell down dead.

The sound of its death came after.

Montag, lying there, eyes gritted shut with dust, a fine wet cement of dust in his now-shut mouth, gasping and crying, now thought again, I remember, I remember, I remember something else. What is it? Yes, yes, part of Ecclesiastes. Part of Ecclesiastes and Revelation. Part of that book, part of it, quick now, quick, before it gets away, before the shock wears off, before the wind dies. Book of Ecclesiastes. Here. He said it over to himself silently, lying flat to the trembling earth, he said the words of it many times and they were perfect without trying and there was no Denham's Dentifrice anywhere, it was just the Preacher by himself, standing there in his mind, looking at him . . .

"There," said a voice.

The men lay gasping like fish laid out on the grass. They held to the earth as children hold to familiar things, no matter how cold or dead, no matter what has happened or will happen, their fingers were clawed into the dirt, and they were all shouting to keep their eardrums from bursting, to keep their sanity from bursting, mouths open, Montag shouting with them, a protest against the wind that ripped their faces and tore at their lips, making their noses bleed.

Montag watched the great dust settle and the great silence move down upon their world. And lying there it seemed that he saw every single grain of dust and every blade of grass and that he heard every cry and shout and whisper going up in the world now. Silence fell down in the sifting dust, and all the leisure they might need to look around, to gather the reality of this day into their senses.

Montag looked at the river. We'll go on the river. He looked at the old railroad tracks. Or we'll go that way. Or we'll walk on the highways now, and we'll have time to put things into ourselves. And someday, after it sets in us a long time, it'll come out our hands and our mouths. And a lot of it will be wrong, but just enough of it will be right. We'll just start walking today and see the world and the way the world walks around and talks, the way it really looks. I want to see everything now. And while none of it will be me when it goes in, after a while it'll all gather together inside and it'll be me. Look at the world out there, my God, my God, look at it out there, outside me, out there beyond my face and the only way to really touch it is to put it where it's finally me, where it's in the blood, where it pumps around a thousand times ten thousand a day. I get hold of it so it'll never run off. I'll hold onto the world tight someday. I've got one finger on it now; that's a beginning.

The wind died.

The other men lay awhile, on the dawn edge of sleep, not yet ready to rise up and begin the day's obligations, its fires and foods, its thousand details of putting foot after foot and hand after hand. They lay blinking their dusty eyelids. You could hear them breathing fast, then slower, then slow . . .

Montag sat up.

He did not move any farther, however. The other

men did likewise. The sun was touching the black horizon with a faint red tip. The air was cold and smelled of a coming rain.

Silently, Granger arose, felt of his arms and legs, swearing, swearing incessantly under his breath, tears dripping from his face. He shuffled down to the river to look upstream.

"It's flat," he said, a long time later. "City looks like a heap of baking powder. It's gone." And a long time after that: "I wonder how many knew it was coming? I wonder how many were surprised?"

And across the world, thought Montag, how many other cities dead? And here in our country, how many? A hundred, a thousand?

Someone struck a match and touched it to a piece of dry paper taken from his pocket, and shoved this under a bit of grass and leaves, and after a while added tiny twigs which were wet and sputtered but finally caught, and the fire grew larger in the early morning as the sun came up and the men slowly turned from looking upriver and were drawn to the fire, awkwardly, with nothing to say, and the sun colored the back of their necks as they bent down.

Granger unfolded an oilskin with some bacon in it. "We'll have a bite. Then we'll turn around and walk upstream. They'll be needing us up that way."

Someone produced a small frying pan and the bacon went into it and the frying pan was set on the fire. After a moment the bacon began to flutter and dance in the pan and the sputter of it filled the morning air with its aroma. The men watched this ritual silently.

Granger looked into the fire. "Phoenix."

"What?"

"There was a silly damn bird called a phoenix back before Christ, every few hundred years he built a pyre and burnt himself up. He must have been first cousin to Man. But every time he burnt himself up he sprang out of the ashes, he got himself born all over again. And it looks like we're doing the same thing, over and over, but we've got one damn thing the phoenix never had. We know the damn silly thing we just did. We know all the damn silly things we've done for a thousand years and as long as we know that and always have it around where we can see it, someday we'll stop making the goddamn funeral pyres and jumping in the middle of them. We pick up a few more people that remember every generation."

He took the pan off the fire and let the bacon cool and they ate it, slowly, thoughtfully.

"Now, let's get on upstream," said Granger. "And hold onto one thought: You're not important. You're not anything. Someday the load we're carrying with us may help someone. But even when we had the books on hand, a long time ago, we didn't use what we got out of them. We went right on insulting the dead. We went right on spitting in the graves of all the poor ones who died before us. We're going to meet a lot of lonely people in the next week and the next month and the next year. And when they ask us what we're doing, you can say, We're remembering. That's where we'll win out in the long run. And someday we'll remember so much that we'll build the biggest goddamn steamshovel in history and dig the biggest grave of all time and shove war in and cover it up. Come on now, we're going to go build a mirror factory first and put out nothing but mirrors for the next year and take a long look in them."

They finished eating and put out the fire. The day was brightening all about them as if a pink lamp had been given more wick. In the trees, the birds that had flown away quickly now came back and settled down.

Montag began walking and after a moment found that the others had fallen in behind him, going north. He was surprised, and moved aside to let Granger pass, but Granger looked at him and nodded him on. Montag went ahead. He looked at the river and the sky and the rusting track going back down to where the farms lay, where the barns stood full of hay, where a lot of people had walked by in the night on their way from the city. Later, in a month or six months, and certainly not more than a year, he would walk along here again, alone, and keep right on going until he caught up with the people.

But now there was a long morning's walk until noon, and if the men were silent it was because there was everything to think about and much to remember. Perhaps later in the morning, when the sun was up and had warmed them, they would begin to talk, or just say the things they remembered, to be sure they were there, to be absolutely certain that things were safe in them. Montag felt the slow stir of words, the slow simmer. And when it came his turn, what could he say, what could he offer on a day like this, to make the trip a little easier? To everything there is a season. Yes. A time to break down, and a time to build up. Yes. A time to keep silence, and a time to speak. Yes, all that. But what else. What else? Something, something . . .

And on either side of the river was there a tree of

life, which bare twelve manner of fruits, and yielded her fruit every month; And the leaves of the tree were for the healing of the nations.

Yes, thought Montag, that's the one I'll save for noon. For noon . . .

When we reach the city.

Author's Afterword

About two years ago, a letter arrived from a solemn young Vassar lady telling me how much she enjoyed reading my experiment in space mythology, *The Martian Chronicles*.

But, she added, wouldn't it be a good idea, this late in time, to rewrite the book inserting more women's characters and roles?

A few years before that I got a certain amount of mail concerning the same Martian book complaining that the blacks in the book were Uncle Toms and why didn't I "do them over"?

Along about then came a note from a Southern white suggesting that I was prejudiced in favor of the blacks and the entire story should be dropped.

Two weeks ago my mountain of mail delivered forth a pipsqueak mouse of a letter from a well-known publishing house that wanted to reprint my story "The Fog Horn" in a high school reader.

In my story, I had described a lighthouse as having, late at night, an illumination coming from it that was a "God-Light." Looking up at it from the viewpoint of any sea-creature one would have felt that one was in "the Presence."

The editors had deleted "God-Light" and "in the Presence."

Some five years back, the editors of yet another anthology for school readers put together a volume with some 400 (count 'em) short stories in it. How do you cram 400 short stories by Twain, Irving, Poe, Maupassant and Bierce into one book?

Simplicity itself. Skin, debone, demarrow, scarify, melt, render down and destroy. Every adjective that counted, every verb that moved, every metaphor that weighed more than a mosquito—out! Every simile that would have made a sub-moron's mouth twitch—gone! Any aside that explained the two-bit philosophy of a first-rate writer—lost!

Every story, slenderized, starved, bluepenciled, leeched and bled white, resembled every other story. Twain read like Poe read like Shakespeare read like Dostoevsky read like—in the finale—Edgar Guest. Every word of more than three syllables had been razored. Every image that demanded so much as one instant's attention—shot dead.

Do you begin to get the damned and incredible picture?

How did I react to all of the above?

By "firing" the whole lot.

By sending rejection slips to each and every one.

By ticketing the assembly of idiots to the far reaches of hell.

The point is obvious. There is more than one way to burn a book. And the world is full of people running about with lit matches. Every minority, be it Baptist/ Unitarian, Irish/Italian/Octogenarian/Zen Buddhist, Zionist/Seventh-day Adventist, Women's Lib/Republican, Mattachine/Four Square Gospel feels it has the will, the right, the duty to douse the kerosene, light the fuse. Every dimwit editor who sees himself as the source of all dreary blanc-mange plain porridge unleavened literature, licks his guillotine and eyes the neck of any author who dares to speak above a whisper or write above a nursery rhyme.

Fire-Captain Beatty, in my novel *Fahrenheit 451*, described how the books were burned first by minorities, each ripping a page or a paragraph from this book, then that, until the day came when the books were empty and the minds shut and the libraries closed forever.

"Shut the door, they're coming through the window, shut the window, they're coming through the door," are the words to an old song. They fit my life-style with newly arriving butcher/censors every month. Only six weeks ago, I discovered that, over the years, some cubbyhole editors at Ballantine Books, fearful of contaminating the young, had, bit by bit, censored some 75 separate sections from the novel. Students, reading the novel which, after all, deals with censorship and book-burning in the future, wrote to tell me of this exquisite irony. Judy-Lynn Del Rey, one of the new Ballantine editors, is having the entire book reset and republished this summer with all the damns and hells back in place.

A final test for old Job II here: I sent a play, *Leviathan 99*, off to a university theater a month ago. My play is based on the "Moby Dick" mythology, dedicated to Melville, and concerns a rocket crew and a blind space captain who venture forth to encounter a Great White Comet and destroy the destroyer. My drama premieres as an opera in Paris this autumn. But, for now, the university wrote back that they hardly dared do my play —it had no women in it! And the ERA ladies on campus would descend with ballbats if the drama department even tried!

Grinding my bicuspids into powder, I suggested that would mean, from now on, no more productions of *Boys in the Band* (no women), or *The Women* (no men). Or, counting heads, male and female, a good lot of Shakespeare that would never be seen again, especially if you count lines and find that all the good stuff went to the males!

I wrote back maybe they should do my play one week, and *The Women* the next. They probably thought I was joking, and I'm not sure that I wasn't.

For it is a mad world and it will get madder if we allow the minorities, be they dwarf or giant, orangutan or dolphin, nuclear-head or water-conservationist, pro-computerologist or Neo-Luddite, simpleton or sage, to interfere with aesthetics. The real world is the playing ground for each and every group, to make or unmake laws. But the tip of the nose of my book or stories or poems is where their rights end and my territorial imperatives begin, run and rule. If Mormons do not like my plays, let them write their own. If the Irish hate my Dublin stories, let them rent typewriters. If teachers and grammar school editors find my jawbreaker sentences shatter their mushmilk teeth, let them eat stale cake dunked in weak tea of their own ungodly manufacture. If the Chicano intellectuals wish to re-cut my "Wonderful Ice Cream Suit" so it shapes "Zoot," may the belt unravel and the pants fall.

For, let's face it, digression is the soul of wit. Take philosophic asides away from Dante, Milton or Hamlet's father's ghost and what stays is dry bones. Laurence Sterne said it once: Digressions, incontestably, are the

sunshine, the life, the soul of reading! Take them out and
one cold eternal winter would reign in every page. Restore
them to the writer—he steps forth like a bridegroom, bids
all-hail, brings in variety and forbids the appetite to fail.

In sum, do not insult me with the beheadings, finger-
choppings or the lung-deflations you plan for my works.
I need my head to shake or nod, my hand to wave or
make into a fist, my lungs to shout or whisper with. I
will not go gently onto a shelf, degutted, to become a
non-book.

All you umpires, back to the bleachers. Referees, hit
the showers. It's my game. I pitch, I hit, I catch. I run
the bases. At sunset I've won or lost. At sunrise, I'm out
again, giving it the old try.

And no one can help me. Not even you.